PHILIP PULLMAN

THE GOLDEN COMPASS
THE GRAPHIC NOVEL

VOLUME ONE

Adapted by Stéphane Melchior, art by Clément Oubrerie
Coloring by Clément Oubrerie with Philippe Bruno
Translated by Annie Eaton

ALFRED A. KNOPF ✦ NEW YORK

THIS IS A BORZOI BOOK PUBLISHED BY ALFRED A. KNOPF

This is a work of fiction. Names, characters, places, and incidents either are the product of the author's imagination or are used fictitiously. Any resemblance to actual persons, living or dead, events, or locales is entirely coincidental.

All rights reserved. Published in the United States by Alfred A. Knopf, an imprint of Random House Children's Books, a division of Penguin Random House LLC, New York. This graphic novel was originally published in French as *Les Royaumes du Nord 1* by Gallimard Jeunesse, Paris, in 2014. *Les Royaumes du Nord 1* copyright © 2014 by Gallimard Jeunesse. Adapted from the English-language work *The Golden Compass* published by Alfred A. Knopf, an imprint of Random House Children's Books, a division of Penguin Random House LLC, in 1995. *The Golden Compass* copyright © 1995 by Philip Pullman.

Knopf, Borzoi Books, and the colophon are registered trademarks of Penguin Random House LLC.

Visit us on the Web! randomhousekids.com

Educators and librarians, for a variety of teaching tools, visit us at RHTeachersLibrarians.com

Library of Congress Cataloging-in-Publication Data available upon request.

MANUFACTURED IN CHINA
September 2015
10 9 8 7 6 5 4 3 2 1

First U.S. Edition

Random House Children's Books supports the First Amendment and celebrates the right to read.

OXFORD

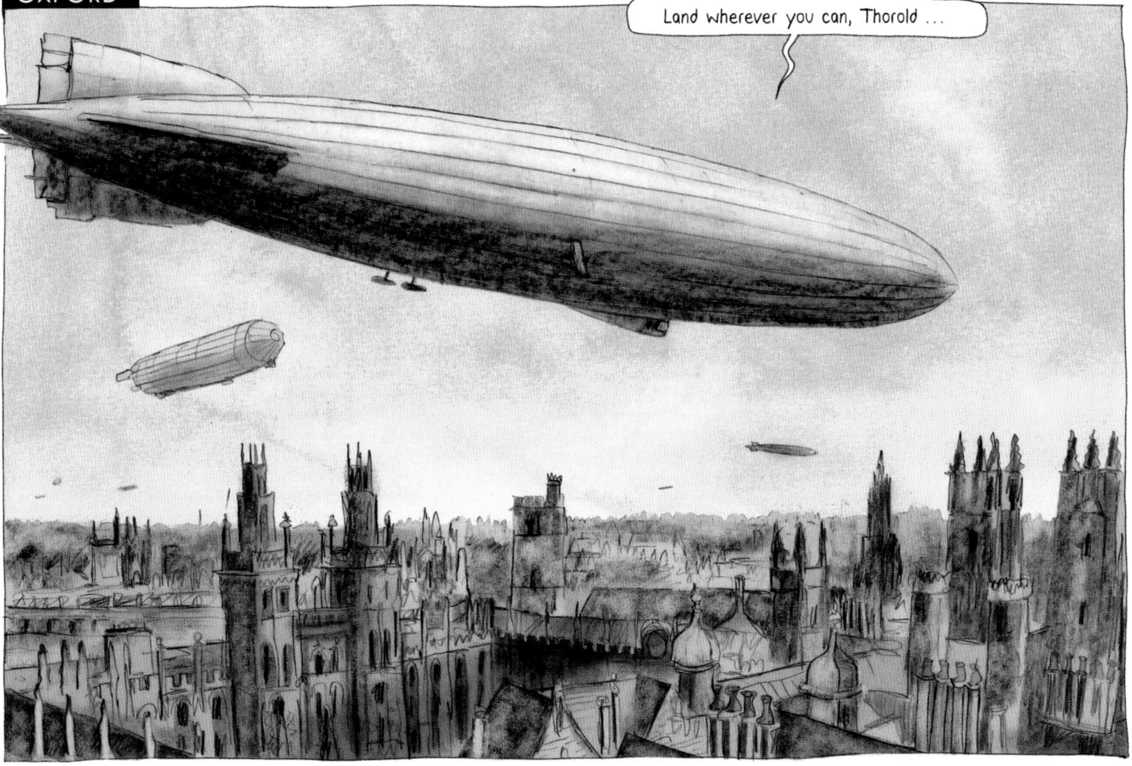
Land wherever you can, Thorold ...

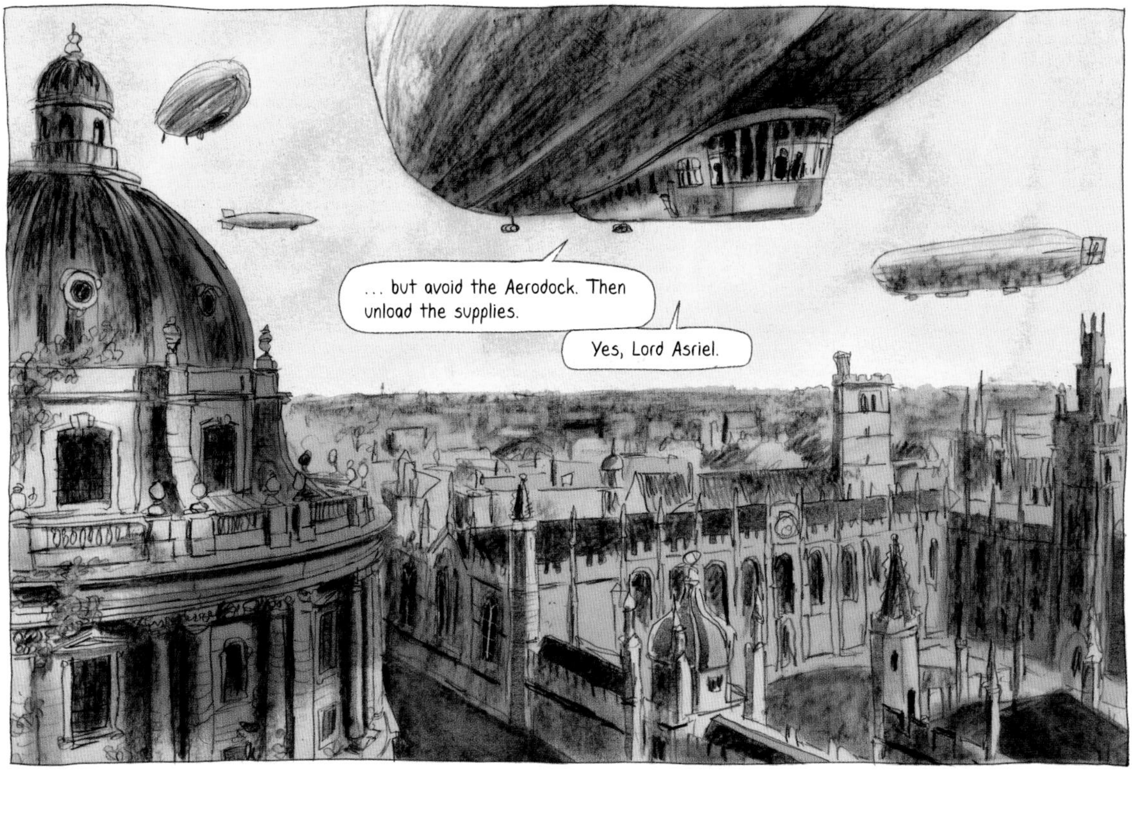
... but avoid the Aerodock. Then unload the supplies.
Yes, Lord Asriel.

Master, Wren is here with the wine.

Tokay 1898.

Lord Asriel is very partial to it.

Good, now put it down and leave us.

Would it hurt you to say thanks?

You forget who you're talking to!

Thank you, Wren. You may go.

Did you see that?

The Master's not in a good mood, Pan.

He'll be in an even worse mood if he catches you here.

I'm not scared of him.

Liar!

I've had enough of Jordan College. I feel as if I've been here forever.

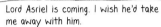

Lord Asriel is coming. I wish he'd take me away with him.

Your uncle is even scarier than the Master.

Look!

?

Poison!

Are you mad?

Why are you always imagining things?

Come!

Let's go and greet Lord Asriel when he arrives.

Phew! It's a relief to stretch our legs!

Let's go!

I know there's stuff going on at the moment ...

political stuff!

You don't know what you're talking about! Quick, let's go!

Why would they want to kill Lord Asriel?

You don't know it's poison.

It could be medicine. The Master could have heartburn.

Of course it's poison.

Otherwise the Master wouldn't have asked Wren to leave the room before he poured it in.

You're right.

It's poison. All the more reason for us to get out of here.

Certainly I am!

Coward!

The Master's cigars!

Promise me that as soon as he leaves, we'll go too!

Well, well, Wren?!

Lord Asriel! How long have you been here?

A little while.

The Master is waiting for you at the Aerodock. You must have missed him.

We like to show up where we're least expected.

You can leave us, Wren, unless you're waiting for the Master to arrive so that he can offer you a cigar?

Your favorite wine is in the carafe. Welcome to Jordan College, my lord.

What a hypocrite. Do you think he's in on it?

You know absolutely nothing about anything.

We must stop him from drinking.

If your uncle finds us spying on him, he'll skin us alive.

No!

?!

Lyra!

So is that what they're teaching you here? Spying?

Ouch, that hurts!

The wine! It's poisoned!

A spy and a liar. They've really done well with your education.

I was hiding! I saw!

The Master poured powder into the wine.

The Master, eh?

?!

Here's our plan: you go back into your hiding place, and later you can tell me everything you've seen.

WELL DONE! Because of you, we're back in this rat hole.

This time it's different. We're on a mission: he said "our plan"!

I'm sure he'll take me with him.

Why would you want that? He scares me.

Pan, you're a coward.

And you're reckless.

SHUT UP, BOTH OF YOU, OR I'LL MAKE YOU WISH YOU WERE DEAD!

Set the lantern up here, Thorold, and we'll have the screen in front of the window.

It's hot in here.

This isn't the moment to fall asleep.

Don't worry....

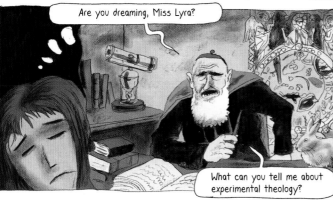

Are you dreaming, Miss Lyra?

What can you tell me about experimental theology?

That ...

... it's boring.

But ...

Come back, you little savage!

LONG LIVE SAVAGES!

In God's name, Lyra!

Get down from there!

He who swears will go to hell, Mr. Parslow!

What's the use of learning? There are more books than I could ever read here.

That's what it's like in all libraries, Lyra.

They all claim to believe in God, and yet they keep searching for him with their philosophical instruments.

If the Chaplain could hear you!

LYRA! COME BACK TO YOUR LESSON IMMEDIATELY OR I'LL TELL THE MASTER!

Ha ha ha!

Miss Lyra! Who gave you permission to leave the college?

I gave myself permission, Mr. Wood.

Why wasn't I told that you had arrived?

Because that's how I wanted it.

Lord Asriel, I'm confused!

Wake up, Lyra.

How is it that ...

I wasn't asleep!

The Master's here.

But ...?!

Ah yes, it was the Tokay.... My fault!

What's all this equipment? I thought your trip was a simple courtesy visit.

Gather the council.

I'm back from the North, and I have something very interesting to show you.

Have you heard? They're saying the Tartars have invaded Muscovy ...

... and they're besieging St. Petersburg. If the city falls, the Tartars could control the Baltic Sea and dominate the whole of Western Europe.

Pan, do you think there's going to be a war?

Not now. Lord Asriel wouldn't be here if war was about to break out next week.

Let's not get distracted. I'd rather save my opinions for the Prime Minister. The matter I wanted to talk to you about, which explains my presence here at Jordan College ...

... is, let's say, of a more essential nature.

See? It was a good idea to come, wasn't it?

Maybe yes, maybe no.

And what's that box? I wonder what's inside it.

As you know, I set out for the North on a diplomatic mission to the king of Lapland. At least that's the reason I gave for the visit.

In fact, my real aim was to go farther north, right onto the ice, to discover what had happened to the Grumman expedition.

The devil! He knew about the wine, I'm sure of it.

Then we'll have to find another way.

You'll recognize Professor Stanislaus Grumman, of course.

That photogram was taken with a standard silver nitrate emulsion.

Here you see it developed with a new, specially prepared emulsion.

That light beside Grumman. Is it going up or coming down?

It's coming down, but it isn't light ...

... it's DUST.

Lord Asriel, you can't be serious?

Dust ... oh!

It can't be....

But how ...

It's heresy!

Explain it to me. I don't understand what's going on. What's this Dust?

I haven't got a clue, but my uncle has the whole council all worked up.

Arguing won't change anything. It's definitely Dust.

Now I'd like you to concentrate on the shape next to Grumman. Here's a close-up....

I thought that was the man's dæmon.

You're missing a detail....

Grumman's dæmon is a serpent, and it was coiled around his neck at the moment the photogram was taken. The shape you can see is a child....

My God! He's right!

It's trickery! Shhh!

It's horrible. A severed child ...?

It can't be—look, that child has no legs....

Caw!

IT'S THE GOBBLERS! Look at what they're doing to children.

No, it can't be. You're getting confused.

Calm down! Look more carefully and you'll see that the child is whole. And that's what is interesting, isn't it, given the nature of Dust.

Now I'd like to show you another picture.... What you can see above Grumman's camp is the Aurora Borealis.

We're all familiar with the Northern Lights, Lord Asriel. Surely you've got a more interesting photogram to show us?

OH!

Move, so I can see too!

A CITY!

IN ANOTHER WORLD!

Is this the Barnard-Stokes business? It is, isn't it?

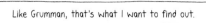

Like Grumman, that's what I want to find out.

Was Dr. Grumman investigating this phenomenon too? If these photograms are in your possession, you must have found him.

He's dead.

Here's the proof.

DID YOU SEE THAT, PAN? BRILLIANT!

Sometimes I find it hard to believe I'm your dæmon.

I found his body preserved in the ice near Svalbard. Look at how carefully his killers scalped their victim.

I'd like to examine that head more closely.

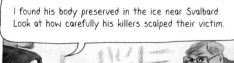

There's a hole at the top of the skull.

Trepanning?

Exactly.

To think that Professor Grumman was once a Scholar of this College.

And to end up like that, in the hands of the Tartars.

The Tartars? Grumman was too far north for that.

The *panserbjørne*, then? You're not serious. The armored bears aren't capable of such an atrocity.

Then you don't know Iofur Raknison, king of Svalbard. A usurper who tricked his way to the throne.

A powerful figure and in no way a fool, in spite of his ludicrous affectations.

They say he's built himself a palace from imported marble, and that he's setting up what he calls a university....

For whom? For the bears?

Ha ha ha

Ha ha ha

Iofur Raknison desires everything that humans have.

Do you know what he wants above all else?

A dæmon! Find a way to give him a dæmon and he'll do anything for you.

We mustn't forget this, Pan.

It's too hot in here. I'm nodding off.

These bear we ought ..

... Wake me up when they've finished.

Bravo!

What a great spy you make!

I ... I wasn't sleeping.

I'm going back to the North, and you need to get to your room and say nothing about this.

No, I'm coming with you.

Your place is here.

But why? I want to see the Northern Lights, the bears, the icebergs, and everything. I want to know about Dust. And that city in the air. Is it really another world?

Get that out of your head. You're not coming with me, child. Do as you're told, and if you're a good girl, I'll bring you back a walrus tusk with Inuit carvings on it.

I spied for you! We're a team!

STOP ARGUING, OR I'M GOING TO LOSE MY TEMPER!

I hope they chop off YOUR head!

I don't know how he knew, but I'm relieved that he smashed the decanter. I never liked the idea of ...

... of murder? No one would like that idea, Charles—even though the alethiometer warns of appalling consequences if Lord Asriel pursues his research. Well, providence saw fit to halt our plan.

Remind me. What is the Barnard-Stokes business?

The Holy Church teaches us that there are two worlds: the world of everything we can see and hear and touch, and another world, the spiritual world of heaven and hell.

Barnard and Stokes were two theologians, let's say ... renegades, who proposed the existence of many other worlds similar to ours, neither heaven nor hell, but material and sinful; close by, but invisible and unreachable.

The Holy Church naturally disapproved of this abominable heresy, and Barnard and Stokes were silenced.

Jordan College has always protected Lord Asriel, and vice versa, but now ...

It's terrible!

And now here's Lord Asriel bringing back a picture, proof of the existence of one of these worlds!

The Magisterium will accuse us of complicity in heresy and—

Hush!

And that's not all. Lyra's going to be drawn into all this, whether I want to protect her or not. The murder of Lord Asriel would only have given us a brief respite.

But how do you know this? The alethiometer again?

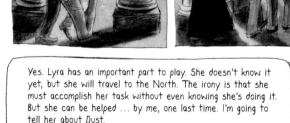

Yes. Lyra has an important part to play. She doesn't know it yet, but she will travel to the North. The irony is that she must accomplish her task without even knowing she's doing it. But she can be helped ... by me, one last time. I'm going to tell her about Dust.

Why would she be interested in an obscure theological enigma?

Because of what she must experience. Part of that includes a great betrayal. Lyra is not just a child, she is THE Child.

Who is going to betray her?

That's the saddest thing. She herself will be the betrayer.

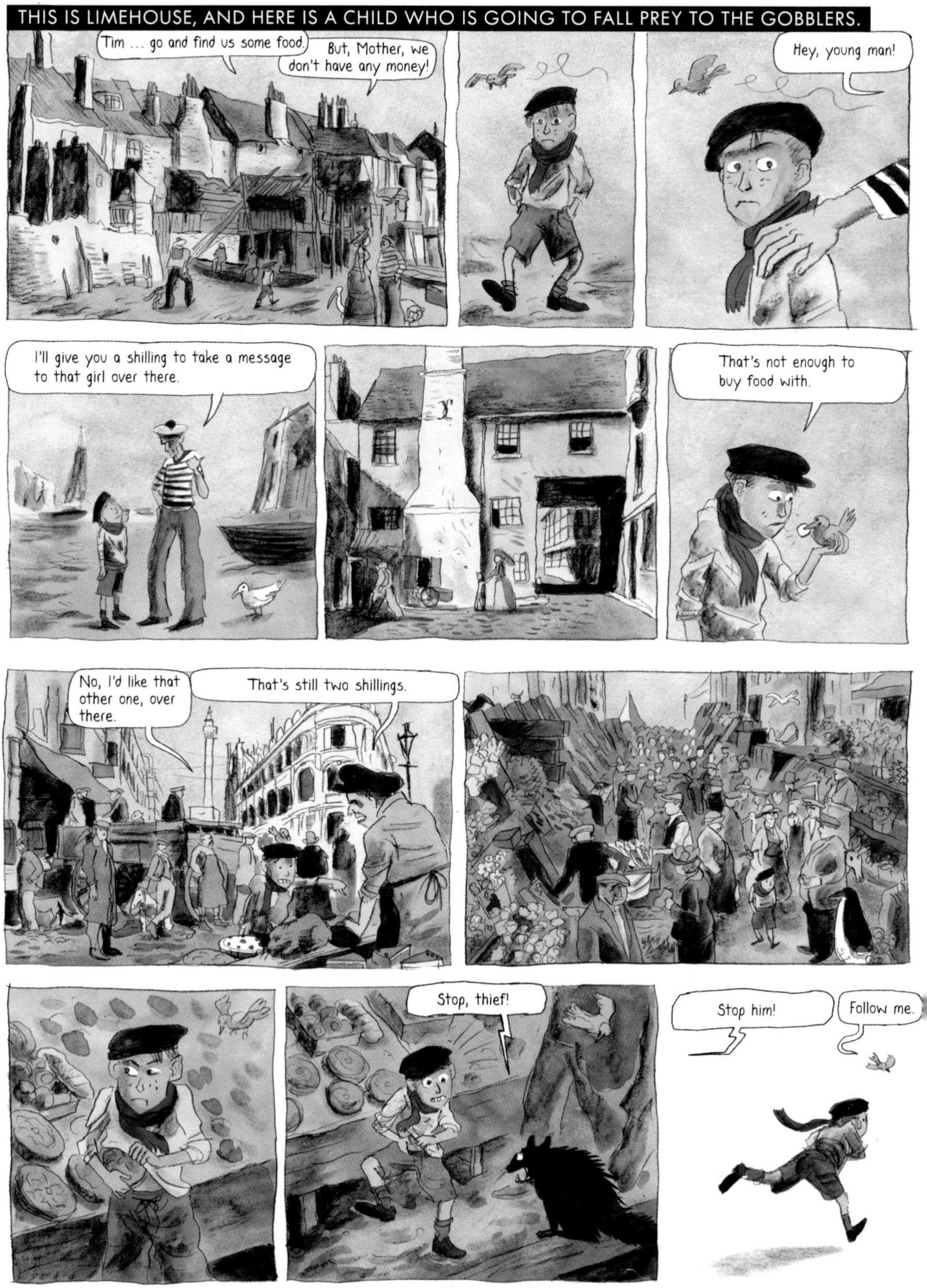
THIS IS LIMEHOUSE, AND HERE IS A CHILD WHO IS GOING TO FALL PREY TO THE GOBBLERS.
Tim ... go and find us some food.
But, Mother, we don't have any money!
Hey, young man!
I'll give you a shilling to take a message to that girl over there.
That's not enough to buy food with.
No, I'd like that other one, over there.
That's still two shillings.
Stop, thief!
Stop him!
Follow me.

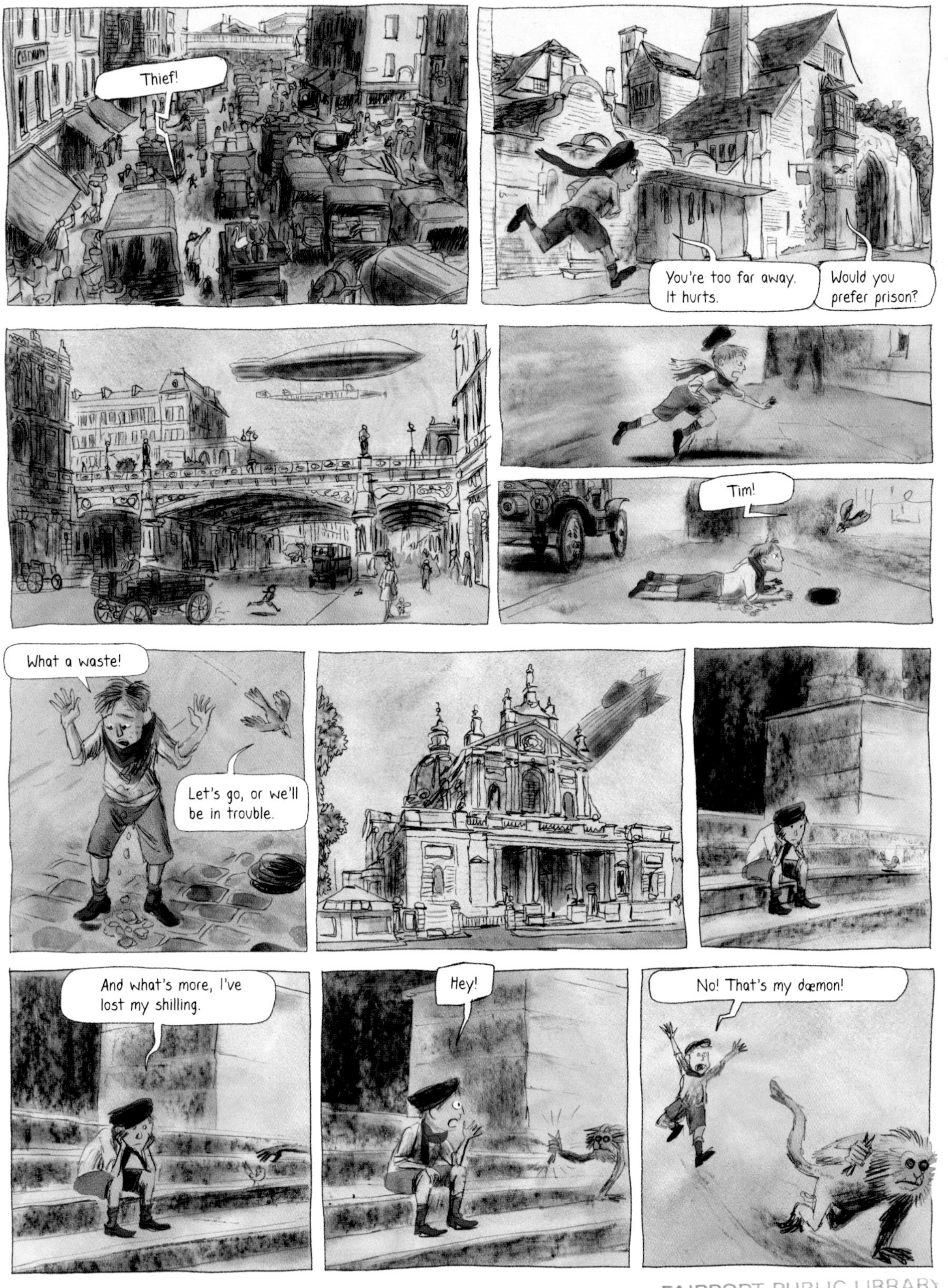
Thief!
You're too far away. It hurts.
Would you prefer prison?
Tim!
What a waste!
Let's go, or we'll be in trouble.
And what's more, I've lost my shilling.
Hey!
No! That's my dæmon!

Roger, let's play kids and Gobblers.

How d'you play that?

You hide; then I find you and slice you open, right, like the Gobblers do.

You don't know what they do.

You're scared, I can tell.

Not as scared as you.

They might not do that at all. They might not even be real.

ROGER!

Aaah!

Brandy. I bet it's the oldest bottle in the world.

Now it's your turn.

I do work in the kitchens. I've drunk this before.

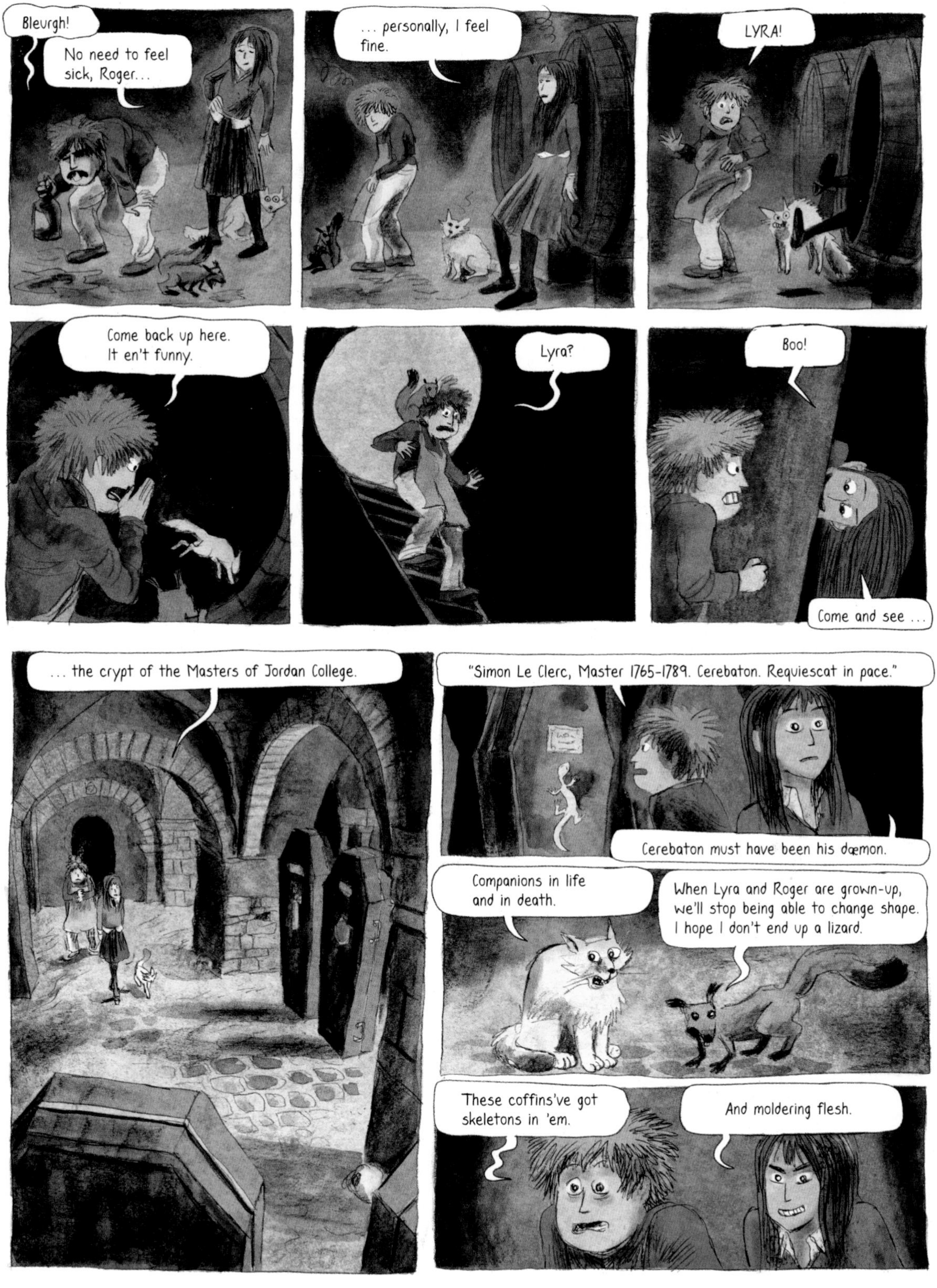

Bleurgh!
No need to feel sick, Roger...
... personally, I feel fine.
LYRA!
Come back up here. It en't funny.
Lyra?
Boo!
Come and see ...
... the crypt of the Masters of Jordan College.
"Simon Le Clerc, Master 1765-1789. Cerebaton. Requiescat in pace."
Cerebaton must have been his dæmon.
Companions in life and in death.
When Lyra and Roger are grown-up, we'll stop being able to change shape. I hope I don't end up a lizard.
These coffins've got skeletons in 'em.
And moldering flesh.

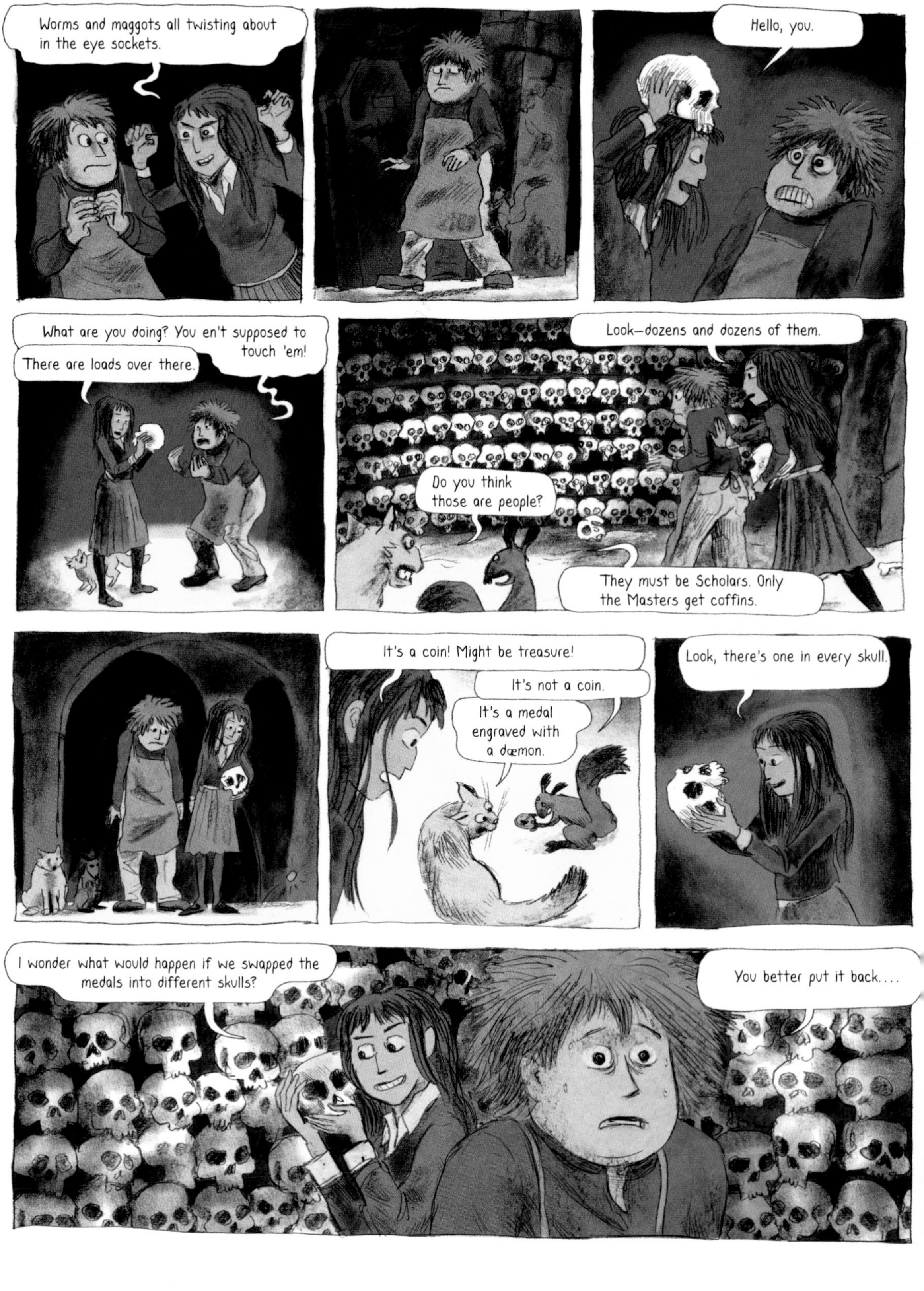
Worms and maggots all twisting about in the eye sockets.
Hello, you.
What are you doing? You en't supposed to touch 'em!
There are loads over there.
Look—dozens and dozens of them.
Do you think those are people?
They must be Scholars. Only the Masters get coffins.
It's a coin! Might be treasure!
It's not a coin.
It's a medal engraved with a dæmon.
Look, there's one in every skull.
I wonder what would happen if we swapped the medals into different skulls?
You better put it back. . . .

LYRAAAAA

Eeeek! Go away!

WOOOOO!

Give us back our dæmons, you little savage.

Roger, come and help me!

It was only a nightmare, but you deserved the punishment.

Your job is in the kitchens, isn't it, Roger?

Yes, Father Intercessor.

Then stay there!

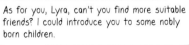

As for you, Lyra, can't you find more suitable friends? I could introduce you to some nobly born children.

Roger's good enough for me.

If there's anything you're worried about, you can always tell me.

I'd rather tell Roger.

Oh, Lord.

Four hundred pounds for this old nag?

Lyra . . .

Promise me we'll never play Gobblers again.

Look. . . .

The gyptians are back.

I don't know what you see in 'em.

They're free.

I don't trust 'em.

I don't trust 'em.

Me neither. Let's go and see them.

Hey. Can I have a go?

Blimey, you've got a nerve turning up after the hiding we gave you last time.

It was more like us giving you a thrashing!

Lyra, can we go, please?

cough! cough!

WHAT HAVE YOU DONE WITH HIM, YOU HALF-ARSED PILLOCK?

I dunno. He was here one minute and gone the next.

HE WAS HOLDING YOUR BLOODY HORSES FOR YOU!

Well, he should've stayed here, then.

Look, I'm not the brat's father!

He does have a father, I suppose?

OI! YOU THERE!

Have you seen my son?

No, Ma Costa.

We don't know where he is.

And you, Miss Fancy. You know Billy, don't you?

Yes, Ma.

Well, go look for him!

Hey!

?!

Stop, thief! My horse!

BILLY!

They say the Gobblers are here.

Yeah, they steal children and eat them....

They swallow them raw—like cannibals.

You don't know. Nobody's ever seen 'em.

I saw them once.

They distracted this lady while another man took her little boy. They put him in a white truck and drove off quick.

They're cannibal pirates.

Well then, what're we waiting for? Let's go and look for 'em! And their white truck!

WE MUST FIND BILLY!

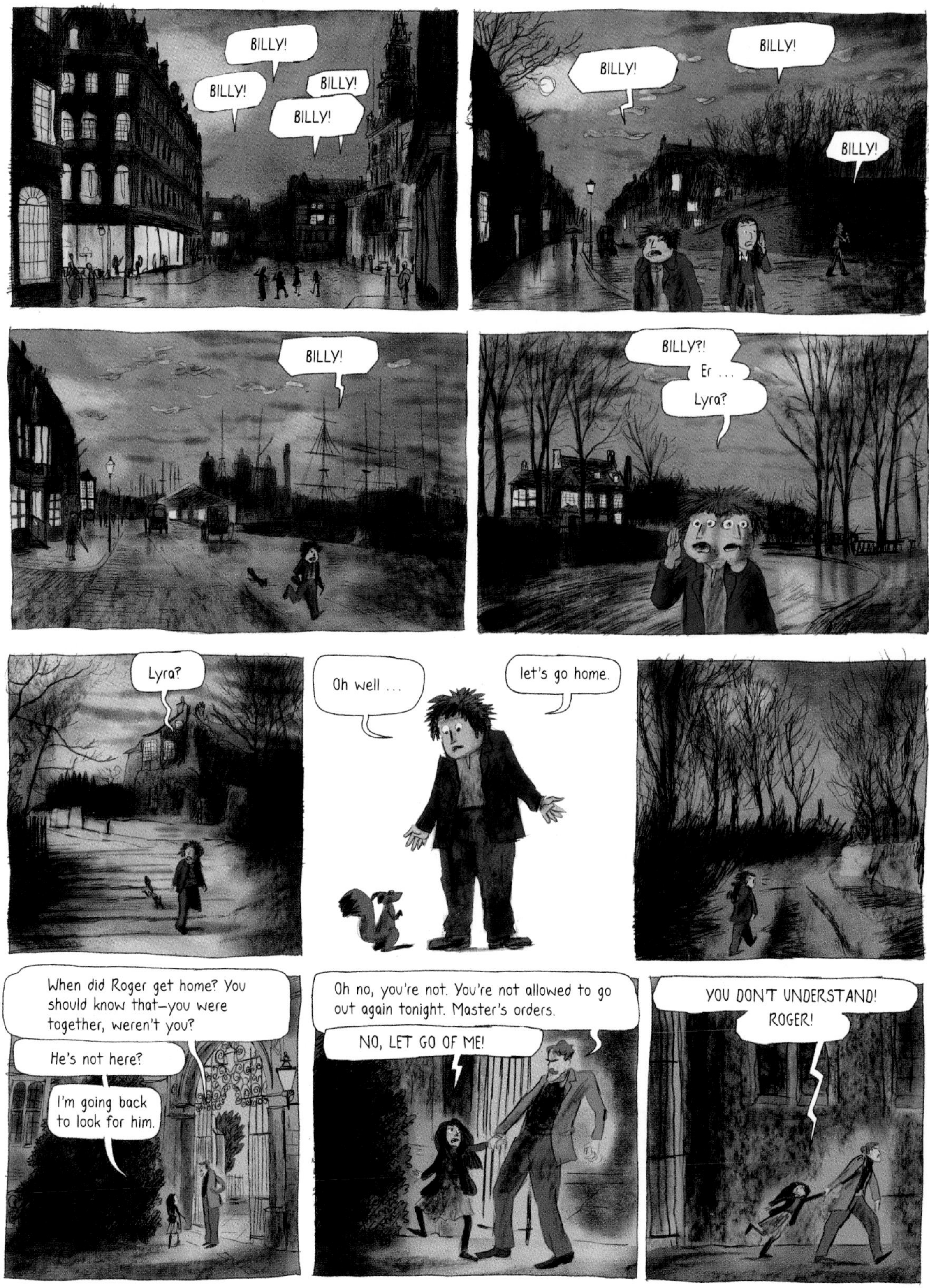
BILLY!
BILLY!
BILLY!
BILLY!
BILLY!
BILLY!
BILLY!
BILLY!
BILLY?!
Er ...
Lyra?
Lyra?
Oh well ...
let's go home.
When did Roger get home? You should know that—you were together, weren't you?
He's not here?
I'm going back to look for him.
Oh no, you're not. You're not allowed to go out again tonight. Master's orders.
NO, LET GO OF ME!
YOU DON'T UNDERSTAND! ROGER!

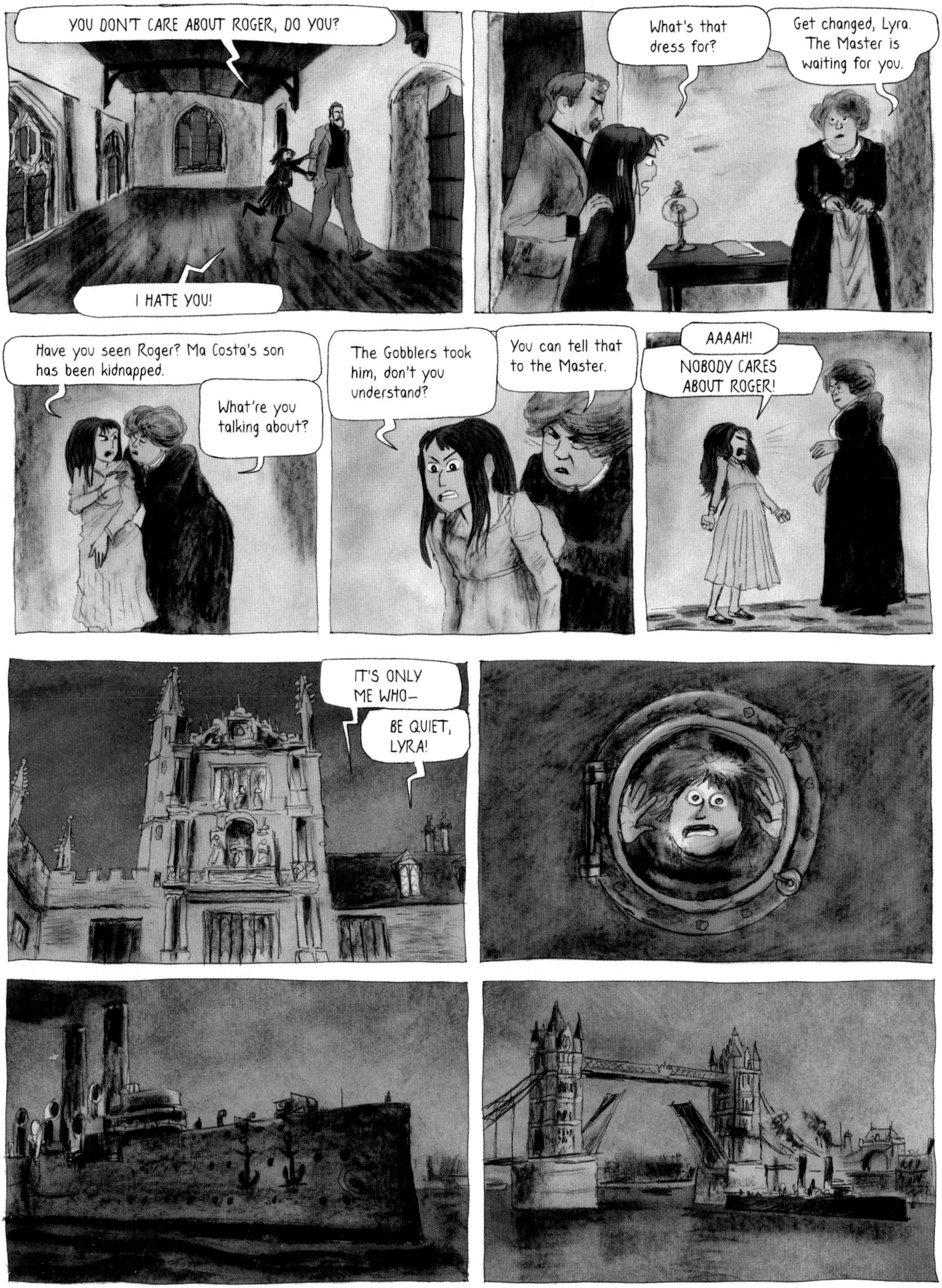
YOU DON'T CARE ABOUT ROGER, DO YOU?
I HATE YOU!
What's that dress for?
Get changed, Lyra. The Master is waiting for you.
Have you seen Roger? Ma Costa's son has been kidnapped.
What're you talking about?
The Gobblers took him, don't you understand?
You can tell that to the Master.
AAAAH!
NOBODY CARES ABOUT ROGER!
IT'S ONLY ME WHO—
BE QUIET, LYRA!

None of that nonsense. Roger is my nephew. He's Mr. Parslow's nephew too. I bet you didn't know that, 'cause I bet you never asked, Miss Lyra.

Don't you chide me with not caring about the boy. I even care about you—though you've given me little enough reason and no thanks.

Good evening, Lyra. I'm glad you could come.

Master ...

... I've got to talk to you about something. It's very important.

Not right now, Lyra.

First of all, I'd like to introduce you to someone.

But—

Mrs. Coulter, this is our Lyra.

Lyra, say hello to Mrs. Coulter.

Good evening, Mrs. Coulter.

Hello, Lyra.

I hope you'll sit next to me at dinner. These receptions can be so dull.

I've never seen you at Jordan College.

Are you a female Scholar?

Not really. I'm a member of Dame Hannah's college.

She's the lady over there with the Master. But most of my work takes place outside Oxford.

Dinner is served.

... and then the ghosts came into my bedroom! But without their heads! Ha ha!

If I hadn't put the medals back the next day, they'd probably have killed me.

I can see you're not afraid of danger, then.

You're the only child living in Jordan College. Don't you ever get lonely?

I had ...
I have a friend....

You're much too young to study at this university. Wouldn't you like to go to school?

The Scholars teach me all I need to know ... when they've got time.

And does your uncle Lord Asriel have plans for you?

He's going to take me to the North ... one day.

Oh, do you know my uncle?

That's true. I remember him telling me—

I met him at the Royal Arctic Institute. Last year I spent three months in Greenland observing the Aurora.

Are you an explorer too?

In a way. Would you like me to tell you about it?

So, Lyra. You've been talking to Mrs. Coulter. Did you enjoy hearing what she said?

Oh yes!

She's the most wonderful person I've ever met....

Quite.

Lyra, you've been safe here in Jordan College. I think you've been happy here. You've not found it easy to be obedient, but we're very fond of you and you've never been a bad child.

There's a great deal of goodness and sweetness in your nature. Lots of determination too. You'll need all of that.

There are things going on in the wide world that I'd have liked to protect you from, by keeping you here in Jordan.

But that's no longer possible.

NO!

No! I don't want to leave Jordan. I like it here. I want to stay here forever.

When you're young, you think that things last forever. Unfortunately, they don't. It won't be long before you become a young woman. You need female company.

I do not!

Not like those female Scholars at dinner, anyway—they smelled of cabbage and mothballs.

But what if it were ...

... Mrs. Coulter?

What?!

She ... knows your uncle well. Lord Asriel is very concerned about your future, and when Mrs. Coulter heard about you, she immediately offered to help.

Do you mean she's going to look after me?

Would you like that?

Oh yes!

In that case, I'll ask her to come and talk to you about it.

By the way ... there's no Mr. Coulter; she's a widow. Her husband died tragically in an accident a few years ago. So bear that in mind before you ask.

So, Lyra ...

I gather I'm going to have a new assistant. I do need your help, as there's a lot of work to do.

I'm not afraid of hard work.

We'll have to travel. It could even be dangerous, especially if we travel to the North.

The ... North?!

That would be wonderful, just what I—

But first you're going to have to work really hard. You'll need to study mathematics, navigation, celestial geography....

If you're going to be my teacher, I want to learn it all.

That's perfect, then.

Now we'll be leaving at dawn tomorrow, on the first zeppelin, so you'd better get to bed.

He's handsome.

There's something weird about her.... Did you see her dæmon?

Be quiet and let me sleep.

Handsome? You're mad—Oh!

Shush.

You just don't want to hear—

Lyra ...

The Master wants to see you.

What, again ...?

Yes, quickly now.

Go as you are and tap at his garden window. He's waiting for you.

tap tap

Good girl. Come in quickly. We haven't got long.

I had to catch you before you saw Mrs. Coulter again.

What's wrong? Aren't I going?

Yes. I can't prevent it.

I'm going to give you something, but you must promise me not to show it to anyone. Will you swear to that?

Yes.

What is it?

An alethiometer.

There are only six in existence in the world. This is one of them. Your uncle brought it here.

But what's it for?

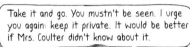

It tells the truth.

You'll have to learn how to read it by yourself somehow. Your uncle—

Are you there, Master?

tap

Take it and go. You mustn't be seen. I urge you again: keep it private. It would be better if Mrs. Coulter didn't know about it.

Quick now, child.

What were you going to say about my uncle?

There isn't time now, Lyra. The powers of this world are very strong. Men and women are moved by tides much fiercer than you can imagine.

Go well, Lyra. Bless you, and, above all, keep your thoughts to yourself.

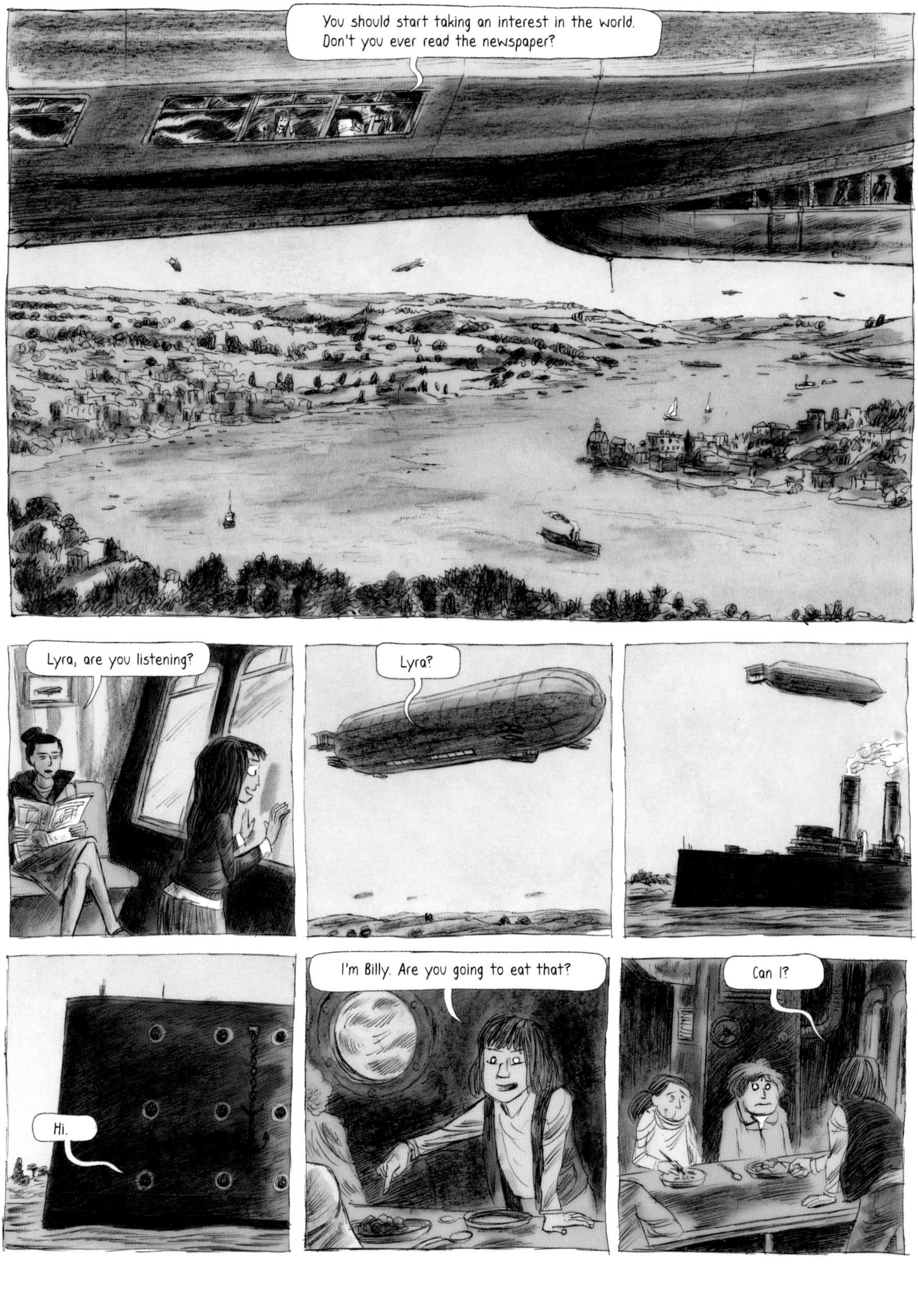
You should start taking an interest in the world. Don't you ever read the newspaper?
Lyra, are you listening?
Lyra?
Hi.
I'm Billy. Are you going to eat that?
Can I?

This is your new home, Lyra.

Is the whole house yours?

No, no.
Only the top floor. I'm a mere explorer.

Pan, look how beautiful it is!

Yes, I can see, Lyra.

And what's that?

Have you never seen a bathroom, Lyra? Then that's where we'll start.

Next I'll take you to the Royal Arctic Institute. I'm one of their few female members.

What's that on your plate?

Seal liver. Try it.

It's as good as calves' liver. But if you're ever stuck for food in the Arctic, you must never eat bear liver.

It's full of a poison that'll kill you in minutes.

Do you see that man in the red tie?

He made the first balloon flight over the North Pole. The other gentleman is Dr. Broken Arrow ...

... a Skraeling who mapped the currents in the Great Northern Ocean.

When are we leaving for the North? You promised we'd go.

And you promised to study hard before we do. Remember?

Let's start here.....

This is the harpoon with which the great whale Grimssdur was killed.

They found the body of Lord Rukh next to this engraved stone, but no Scholar has yet been able to decipher its inscriptions.

Do you really mean it? I can choose?

Better still: you must choose.

I never let anyone else decide for me.

I wish you a very good night, Lyra.

Good night, Mrs. Coulter.

She's gone. Now we can look at the thing.

It's heavy.

It has four hands. So it's not a watch. A compass?

There's a little wheel—look.

No, there are three.

They control the three small hands.

And what about the big hand?

I think it does what it wants.

What do you think the Master was going to say about your uncle?

Maybe that we should give it to him?

But the Master was going to poison him. Perhaps it's the opposite—that we SHOULDN'T give it to him.

No, Pan....

It was her we had to keep it safe from.

Lyra, I should turn the light off now. We'll be busy tomorrow.

All right, Mrs. Coulter.

Good night now.

Good night.

Come in, Lyra.

Here's your teacher, Miss Foster.

But ...

... you promised you would teach me everything yourself.

I haven't got time. I need to prepare for my next expedition.

Our expedition.

Learn your lessons and then we'll see.

... elementary particles ...

Sit up straight! A well-brought-up young lady doesn't slouch.

No, no, and no! A battement and then a tendu. And pay attention to your demi-pointe!

... anbaro-magnetic charges ...

Lyra! A polite young lady drinks without slurping.

Bravo!

Shush!

I shall tell Mrs. Coulter about this!

But ...

... where's my stuff?

Miss Foster tells me you've paid no attention to her lesson on electrons.

She's lying! I know what electrons are.

Let's hear it, then.

Well ... er ... They're negatively charged particles. A bit like Dust, except that Dust isn't charged.

What?!

What did you say? What Dust are you talking about?

You know, from space, that Dust.

It lights people up, if you've got a sort of special camera to see it by.

Except not children. It doesn't affect them.

Do you understand what you're saying? Who did you learn this from?

Oh ... er ... someone at Jordan. A Scholar, I think.

Was it in one of your lessons?

Yes, maybe. Or else it might've been just in passing.

Yes, I think that was it. This Scholar from New Denmark was talking to the Chaplain about it. I just happened to hear it.

We're going to organize a cocktail party.

What for?

Because it'll be fun and your education has skipped over this sort of thing.

We'll buy you a new dress for the occasion, and you can help me with the invitation list. To start with, we absolutely must invite the Archbishop.

He's the most hateful old snob, but I can't afford to leave him out.

But I—

Lord Boreal is in town. And he's such fun.

And what about inviting the Princess Postnikova?

How pretty you look. I'm going to take you to the best hairdresser in London.

This way I'll have it with me all the time. It'll be safer.

What's the point? We won't be going to the North.

She's going to keep us here forever. When are we going to run away?

Why would she be teaching us navigation and all that, if she wasn't going to take us North?

To keep you quiet. You don't really want to stand around at the cocktail party being all sweet and pretty. She's making a pet out of you.

Why are you crying, Lyra?

I'm thinking about Roger.

But what makes me sad is that some days I don't even think about him at all.

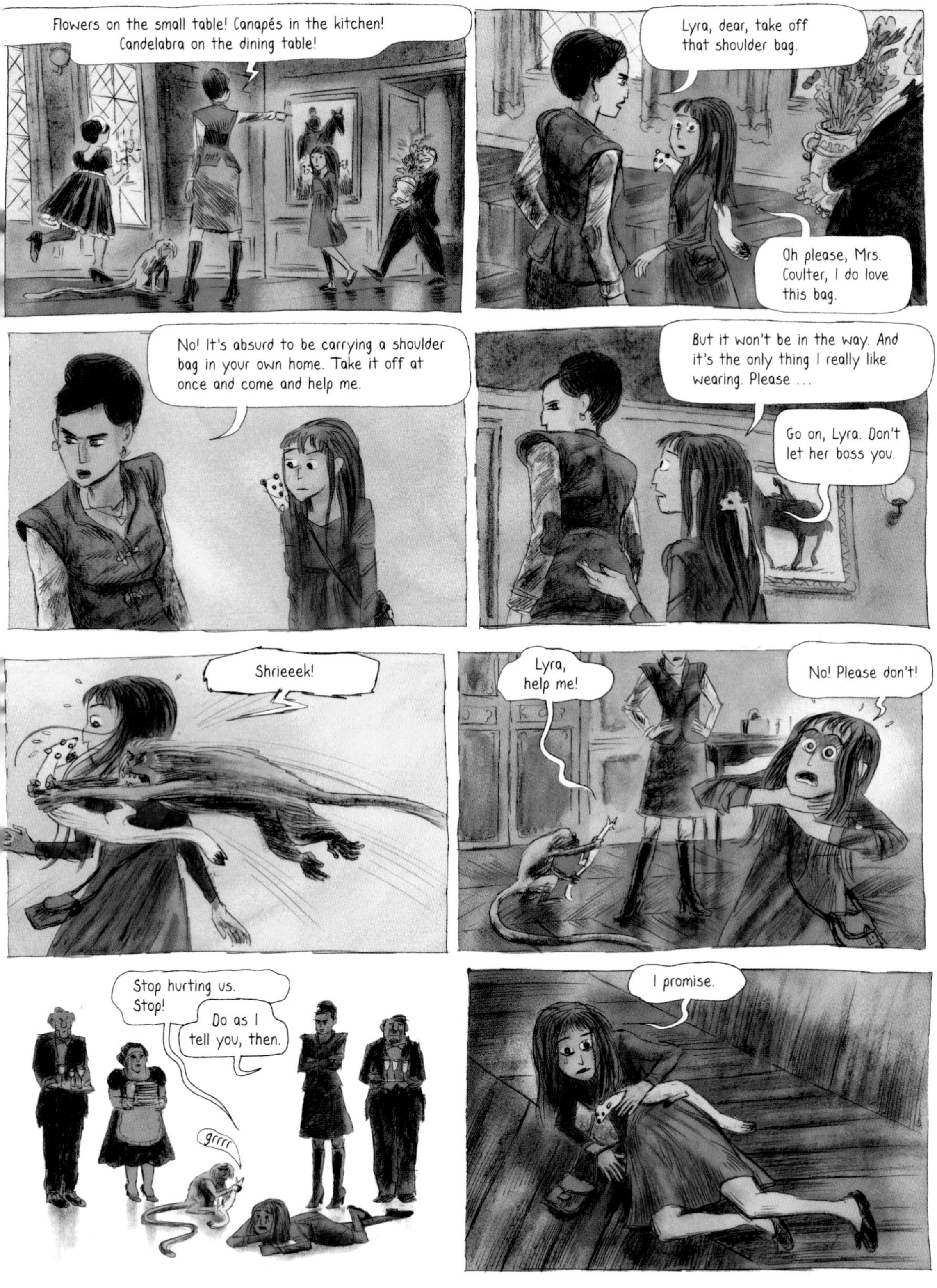
Flowers on the small table! Canapés in the kitchen! Candelabra on the dining table!
Lyra, dear, take off that shoulder bag.
Oh please, Mrs. Coulter, I do love this bag.
No! It's absurd to be carrying a shoulder bag in your own home. Take it off at once and come and help me.
But it won't be in the way. And it's the only thing I really like wearing. Please . . .
Go on, Lyra. Don't let her boss you.
Shrieeek!
Lyra, help me!
No! Please don't!
Stop hurting us. Stop!
Do as I tell you, then.
grrrr
I promise.

So you're the famous Lyra?

A very fine reception your mother has organized.

Oh, she's not my mother!

My parents both died in an aeronautical accident in the North. They were a count and a countess.

Oh, really?

What was your father's name?

Count Belacqua. He was Lord Asriel's brother.

How interesting. And so what are you doing here, then?

I'm here to help. I'm Mrs. Coulter's personal assistant. I'll be accompanying her on her expeditions.

... Dust ...

... attracted by human beings ...

... by adults but not children ...

The General Oblation Board is entirely her own project.

But you, little lady...

... you don't need to be frightened of the General Oblation Board, do you?

Oh, I'm never scared. Not of gyptians who sell children like slaves to the Turks of the Bosphorus. Or of the werewolf at Godstow Priory ...

... not even of the Gobblers.

The Gobblers?

Yes, that's what the tabloids call the General Oblation Board. From the initials, you see.

Why "Oblation," though?

It's an old story. Back in the Middle Ages, parents gave their children to the Church to become monks or nuns. The unfortunate brats were known as "oblates," which means a sacrifice, an offering, something of that sort.

I see. Mrs. Coulter took up the idea again when she became interested in Dust.

More than an idea— it's a passion.

They say the children don't suffer, though.

Why don't you go and have a chat with Lord Boreal?

I'm sure he'd like to meet Mrs. Coulter's young protégée.

Lyra!

I just saw the golden monkey leaving our room. He knows about the alethiometer. He's been spying on us. We've got to escape!

Good evening, child. How is my old friend the Master of Jordan?

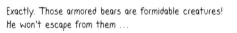

Er, he's very well, thank you.

And your uncle? I've heard that Lord Asriel is being held prisoner in the fortress of Svalbard.

By the armored bears?

Exactly. Those armored bears are formidable creatures! He won't escape from them ...

... even if he lives to be a thousand.

Excuse me, sir. Something urgent's come up.

The bag! We must get the alethiometer back.

Don't worry...

... about that.

You're craftier than a golden monkey. Well done!

Whatever you do, don't look down.

I'm not afraid...

... of anything.

FREE!

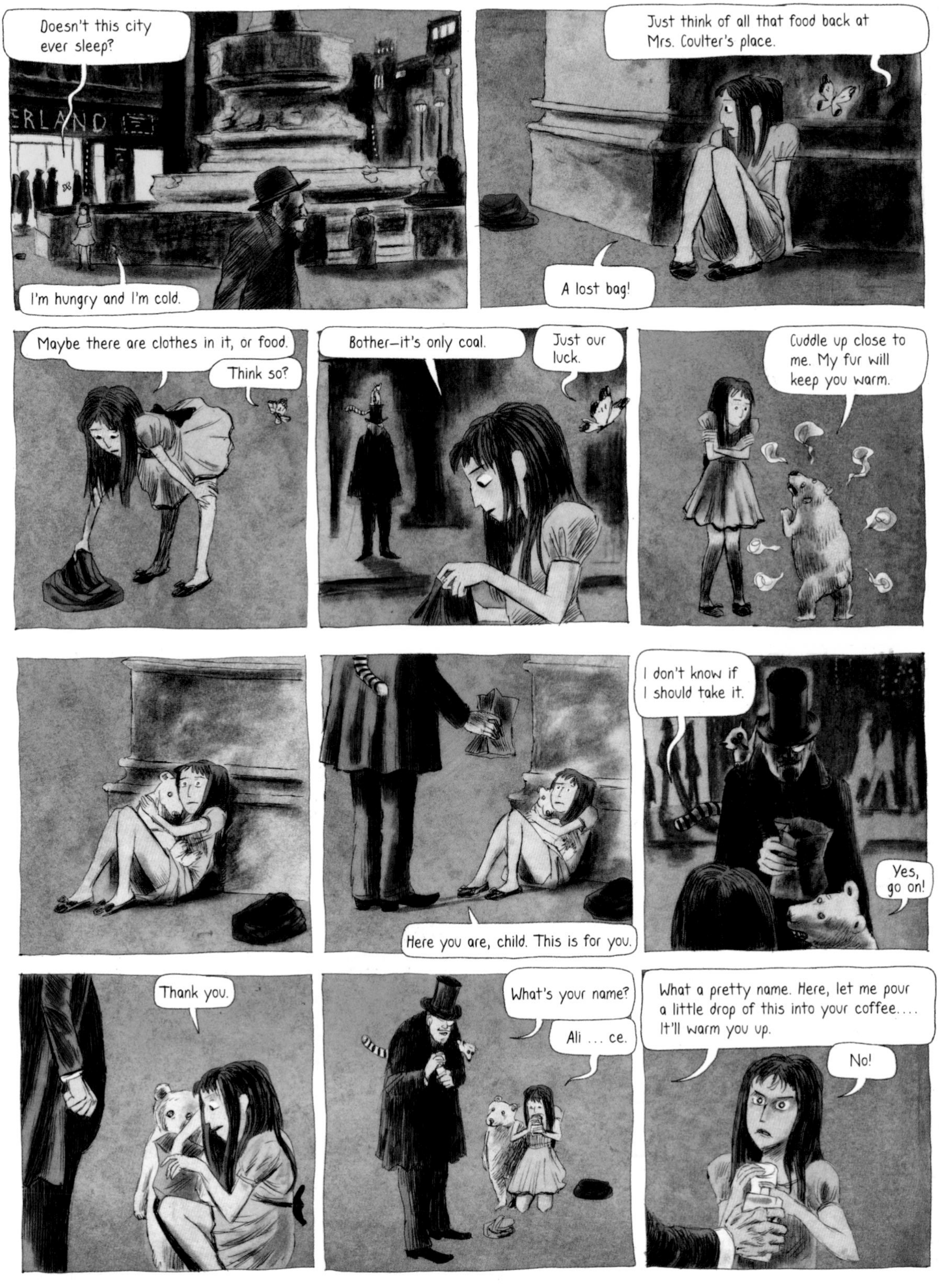
Doesn't this city ever sleep?
ERLAND
I'm hungry and I'm cold.
Just think of all that food back at Mrs. Coulter's place.
A lost bag!
Maybe there are clothes in it, or food.
Think so?
Bother—it's only coal.
Just our luck.
Cuddle up close to me. My fur will keep you warm.
Here you are, child. This is for you.
I don't know if I should take it.
Yes, go on!
Thank you.
What's your name?
Ali . . . ce.
What a pretty name. Here, let me pour a little drop of this into your coffee.... It'll warm you up.
No!

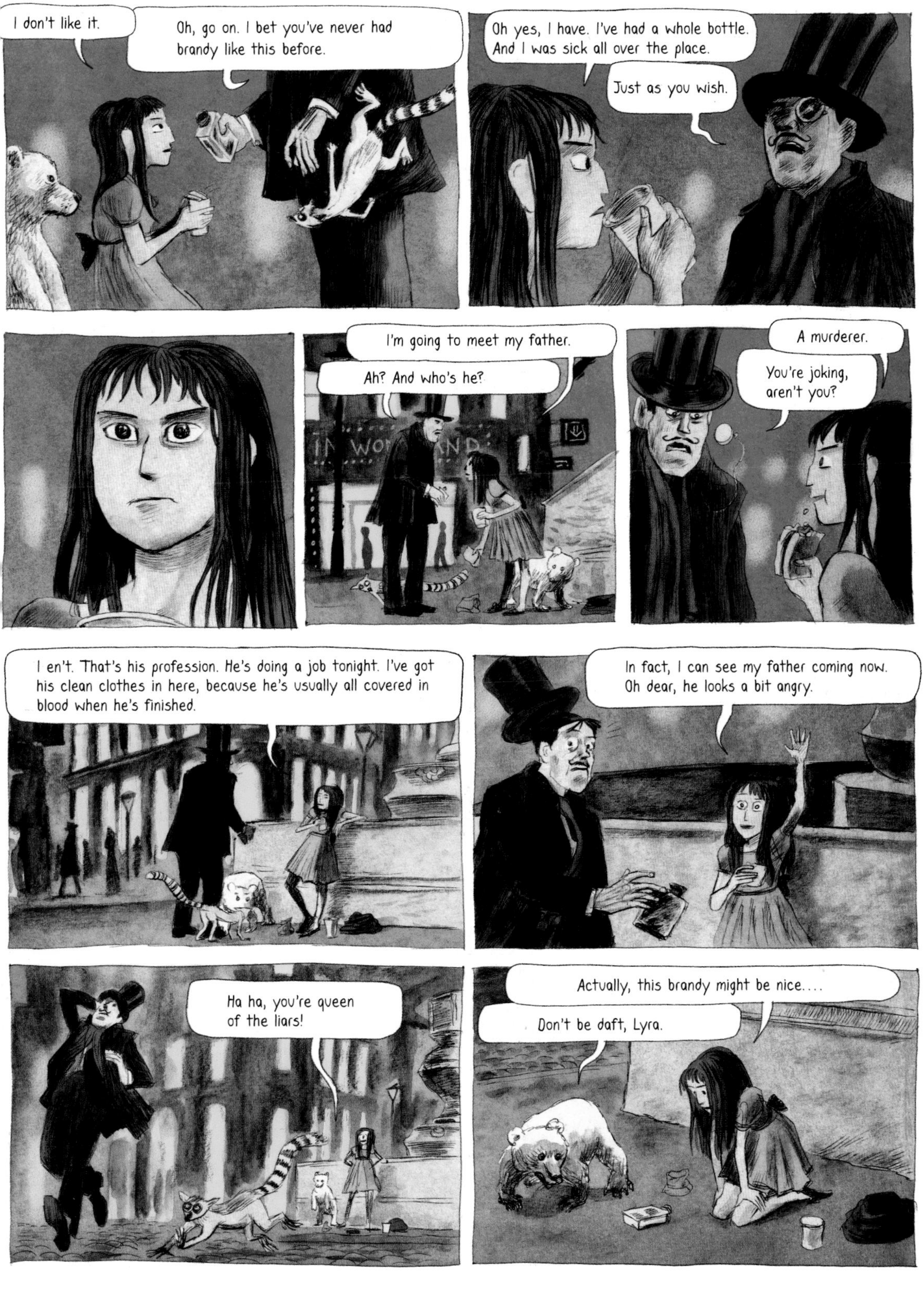
I don't like it.
Oh, go on. I bet you've never had brandy like this before.
Oh yes, I have. I've had a whole bottle. And I was sick all over the place.
Just as you wish.
I'm going to meet my father.
Ah? And who's he?
A murderer.
You're joking, aren't you?
I en't. That's his profession. He's doing a job tonight. I've got his clean clothes in here, because he's usually all covered in blood when he's finished.
In fact, I can see my father coming now. Oh dear, he looks a bit angry.
Ha ha, you're queen of the liars!
Actually, this brandy might be nice....
Don't be daft, Lyra.

Where can we sleep?

Not here, for sure.

Why not sleep under a bridge? That's what they do in stories.

Do you know where there's a bridge? I don't even know what neighborhood we're in.

I think we're heading north.

How do you know? We can't see the stars.

A canal!

And a bridge!

It's Ma Costa, Billy's mother. Maybe she would let us in?

I doubt it. She hates me.

WHAT THE?!

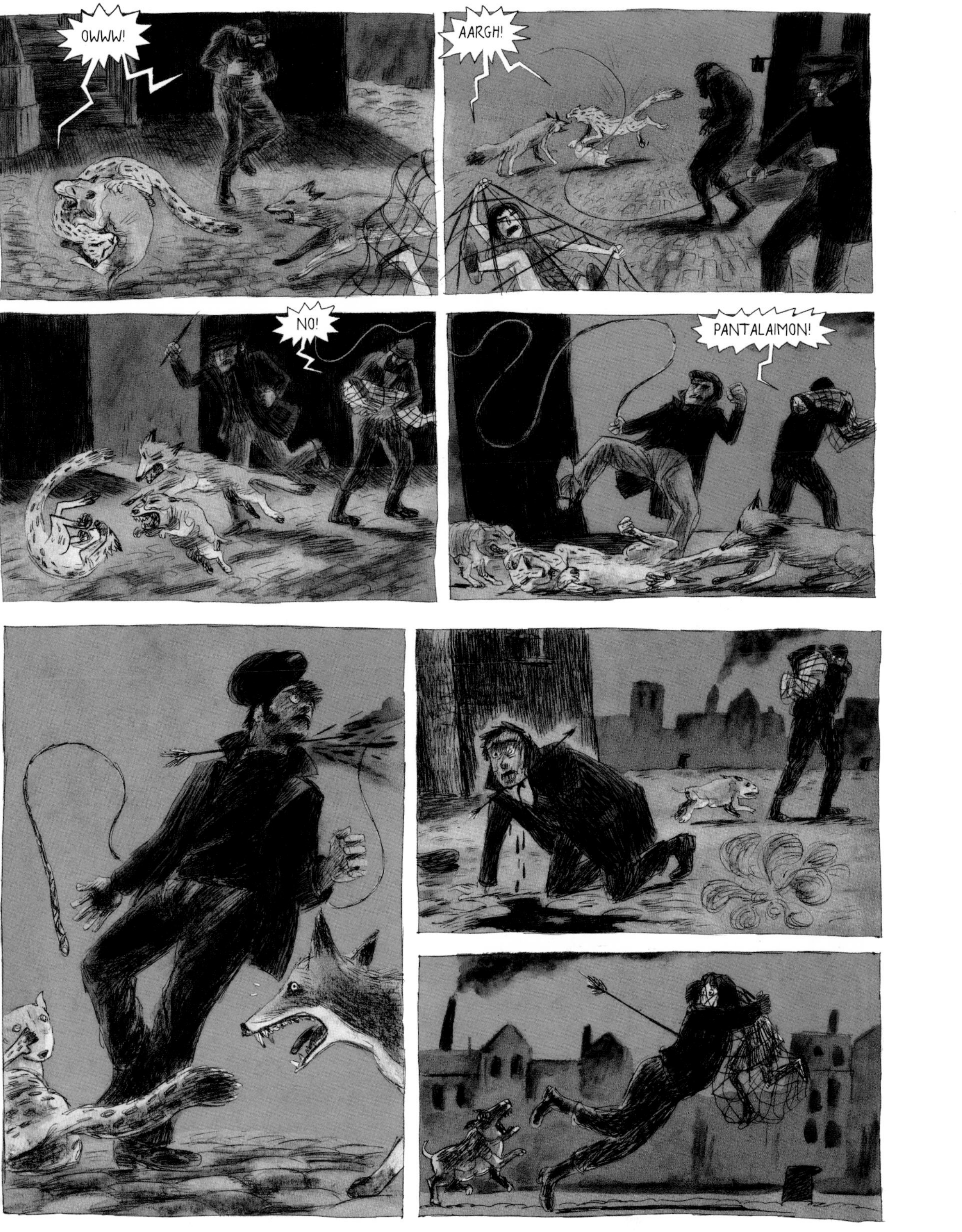
OWWW!
AARGH!
NO!
PANTALAIMON!

Oh, Pan, you were so brave.

I recognized her immediately.

I've been following her since Whitechapel.

Well, well, Lyra . . .

I dunno what you're doing here, but you look wore out.

Sleep, child, and we'll talk tomorrow.

I thought you hated me.

I'm giving you Billy's bunk. Would I be doing that if I hated you?

I'm hungry.

Can it be morning already?

Did you sleep well? Your cabin is lined with cedarwood.

It's supposed to have a soporific effect on dæmons.

Where are we?

Far away. It's important that you stay hidden. I don't want to see you up on deck.

They were Gobblers yesterday, weren't they?

Actually, we thought they'd taken you weeks ago.

They had in a way. I was living with Mrs. Coulter. I think she's in charge of it all.

I think she meant to use me to kidnap more children.

Thank you, Ma.

The Gobblers are taking kids to the far North, to do experiments on 'em.

How do you know that?

We captured a Gobbler and made him talk.

The gyptians have suffered more'n anyone else because of 'em. Right now we're going to meet Lord John Faa, to decide what our next move should be.

Who's John Faa?

He's the king of the gyptians. You'll meet him soon.

Of course, the Tartars of the North eat children....

They never!

Everybody knows.

They just say that so they can take over the fire mines and the coal spirit.

What do you know about the North, little one?

Hey, have you ever heard of the Nälkäinens!

They're a kind of ghost they have up there. Same size as a child, but they've got no heads. They feel their way about at night, and if they get ahold of you, won't nothing make them let go.

And the Windsuckers, they're dangerous too. They drift about in the air. As soon as they touch you, all the strength goes out of you. You can't see 'em except as a kind of shimmer in the air.

And then there are the Breathless Ones, warriors half-killed. They wander about forever because the Tartars have snapped open their ribs and pulled out their lungs. They do it without killing them.

There's an art to it.

And then there's the panserbjørne. Hearda them?

Yes! My uncle is a prisoner in their fortress ... and the Gobblers are pleased, because they're not on his side.

The bears are like mercenaries. They sell their strength to whoever pays them. They're vicious killers, but they keep their word. When you make a bargain with an armored bear, you can rely on it.

Do they make their armor themselves?

Yes. They've got hands as deft as humans. They learned the trick of working with iron way back—meteoric iron mostly.

Are they allies of the Gobblers?

We're not sure. But what I do know is we're going to send a rescue party to free Billy and all the gyptian children.

What about my friend Roger? I have to rescue him. He'd have done the same for me.

Lyra, you can come out now.

These marshes are the fens. The kingdom of the gyptians. You have nothing to fear now.

The Zaal.

The home of the gyptians.

You en't gyptian, Lyra, though you might pass for one.

We're water people, all through, but you're a fire person.

You've got witch oil in your soul. Deceptive, that's what you are, child.

What?!

I en't never deceived anyone! You ask...

It was a compliment, gosling!

HALT!

Are you the little girl what disappeared?

I—

It's her.

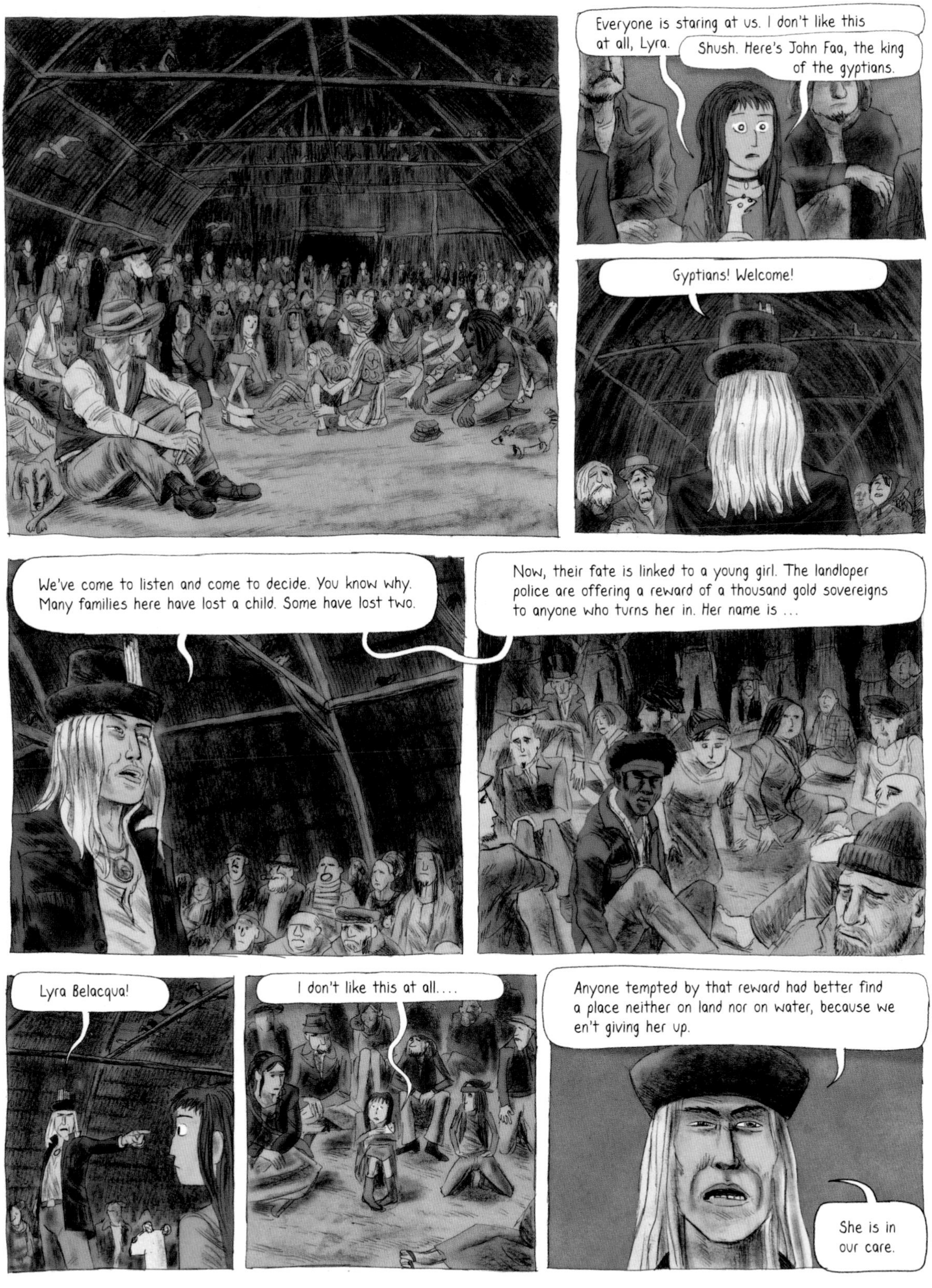
Everyone is staring at us. I don't like this at all, Lyra.
Shush. Here's John Faa, the king of the gyptians.
Gyptians! Welcome!
We've come to listen and come to decide. You know why. Many families here have lost a child. Some have lost two.
Now, their fate is linked to a young girl. The landloper police are offering a reward of a thousand gold sovereigns to anyone who turns her in. Her name is ...
Lyra Belacqua!
I don't like this at all....
Anyone tempted by that reward had better find a place neither on land nor on water, because we en't giving her up.
She is in our care.

The Gobblers are taking their prisoners to a town in the far North, way up in the land of dark.

What's certain is that they're doing it with the support of the police and the clergy. We can trust only ourselves.

What I'm proposing is dangerous. We must send a band of fighters to rescue the children and bring 'em back alive. If we're going to succeed, it will be at great cost to us.

There's landloper kids there too. Are we to rescue them as well?

Are you saying we should fight our way through every kind of danger just to rescue a small group of children and abandon the others? No, you're a better man than that....

Aren't you, Chief Raymond?

Well, my friends, do I have your approval?

HURRAH!

HURRAH!

Can you see any fish?

None.

Then I hope Ma Costa was joking when she said I'd only be eating ...

... what we bring back.

Hey!

You should pay more attention.

Many apologies, Lyra. I'm not as agile as I used to be.

I am Farder Coram, the oldest of the gyptians.

Ma Costa sent you here so that I could talk to you in private. Climb aboard my boat, please.

You won't know this, but I've been interested in your family for a long time. In fact, I know everything about you from the day you were born.

What could there be about me that's so interesting?

What do you know of your origins, Lyra?

Well ... my parents died in an airship accident. That's why Lord Asriel placed me in Jordan College.

Lies.

In truth, your father is ...

... Lord Asriel.

WHAT?!

Sit down, child. You'll tip the boat over.

I'm going to tell you the truth.

When he was a young man, your father went exploring all over the North ...

... and came back with a great fortune. He was a high-spirited, passionate man, quick to anger.

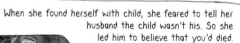

Your mother, she was passionate too. Not as well born as your father, it's true, but very clever and very beautiful.

They fell in love the instant they met. The trouble was, your mother was already married. Her husband was a politician, an important member of the king's party.

When she found herself with child, she feared to tell her husband the child wasn't his. So she led him to believe that you'd died.

Lord Asriel hid you on a farm on his estates and put you under the care of a gyptian woman.

Alas, your mother's husband eventually found out about you and flew into a murderous passion.

He would have killed you and your nurse if your father hadn't intervened.

It was a great scandal.

There was a lawsuit, and Lord Asriel's property was all confiscated.

And your mother wanted nothing to do with him, or with you. The judges took you away from your gyptian nurse, though she begged them not to, and placed you in the care of a priory.

I don't remember any of it.

That's because your father immediately removed you from the priory, and took you to Jordan College and the protection of the Master. The law courts didn't stop him.

Over here!

But then ... who's my mother?

The man Lord Asriel killed was called Edward Coulter.

Mrs. Coulter is my mother?!

That's awful!

She is your mother, and if your father weren't being held by the *panserbjørne*, she would never have dared defy him and you'd still be living at Jordan College.

What the Master was doing letting you go is a mystery I can't explain. He was charged with your care.

I believe the Master tried to keep his promise for as long as he could.

On the night I left, he gave me something. He said my uncle brought it to the College, and he made me promise never to show it to my mother.

I'm happy to show it to you, though.

OH!

The Master told me it was called an alethiometer.

A symbol reader! I never thought I'd set eyes on one again. Do you know how to use it?

I can make the three short hands move.

But I can't do anything with the long one. Except sometimes, if I concentrate very hard, I can make that hand go this way or that, just by thinking it.

Look. All these pictures around the rim are symbols. Take the anchor, there. Its first meaning is hope, for hope holds you fast like an anchor so you don't give way.

But it also means steadfastness, and prevention, as well as the sea, of course.... In fact, for each symbol there's a never-ending series of meanings!

Do you know them all?

I know some. There's a book that explains them all. I've seen it, and I know where it is, but—

JOHN FAA!

You humiliated me in front of my clan and all the gyptian people.

For that, I'm going to kill you!

Many people have tried, Chief Raymond.

Aaagh!

Aaagh!
Don't look, child.
I'm not afraid.
No, John.
Aaagh!
Are we even now?
Yes.
Tomorrow I'll gather all the chiefs of the clans. Make sure you're there.
Where were we?
Ah yes, the symbol reader.
Lord Faa, you're injured. . . .

Thank you, Lyra. Farder Coram, can you tell us how to use the device?

If I remember correctly ...

... you use three hands to ask a question. By pointing to three symbols, you can ask any question you want, since each symbol has so many meanings.

I see.... Then the big hand gives the reply by pointing to other symbols.

But how does the instrument know which question you're thinking of?

It doesn't.

It's up to the questioner to be aware of all the meanings. To do that, you need to have an encyclopedic knowledge or have a very special talent.

The Master must have had a reason to give this rare object to you, child.

What are you thinking, Lyra?

I saw the Master trying to poison Lord Asriel. Why would he have done that?

The Master must have believed that Lord Asriel's discoveries about Dust threatened the College, and perhaps even your own safety. And perhaps the safety of the whole world.

Maybe that's why the Master tried to poison him and entrusted you to your mother, although he'd promised Lord Asriel he wouldn't do that.

But why would he give me the alethiometer?

Since you don't know how to read it, I'll admit I'm foxed.

He said my father presented it to Jordan College in the first place. He was going to say more, but then we were interrupted. I thought he might have wanted me to keep it away from him.

Perhaps.

Or it could be exactly the opposite. Maybe he wanted to make up for trying to kill him.... If you knew how to use the alethiometer, you could probably obtain a lot of answers yourself.

I want to know one last thing, Farder Coram. Who was my gyptian nurse?

HA HA HA!

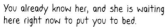

You already know her, and she is waiting here right now to put you to bed.

Ma Costa.

My little one.

Lord Asriel must die.

What sort of poison was it?

A poison from a very rare Turkish serpent.

They catch it by playing a pipe, and then throw it a sponge soaked in honey ...

... and the serpent bites it, but can't get its fangs free, so they can milk the venom out of it.

I'd like to propose a toast to the friendship between Jordan College and the College of Izmir.

But my father had seen what the Turk had done.

And as a sign of that friendship, we will exchange glasses.

The Turkish ambassador was in a fix then, 'cause he couldn't refuse without giving deadly insult.

He had to drink the poison or own up.

Evarghhhh!

It took him five whole minutes to die, and he was in torment all the time.

I saw his body later, when they laid him out. His skin was all withered, like an old apple, and his eyes were starting from his head. In fact, they had to push them back into the sockets.

Ah Lyra—witch's oil in her soul for sure.

Squark!

?!

LYRA! GET BELOW!

It's leaving.

Each picture has several meanings. Why shouldn't I be able to work out what they are? I am Lord Asriel's daughter, after all.

Try harder.

Sometimes when I let my mind wander at the same time as the big hand, I get visions....

I know....
I feel them too.

Thank you, clan chieftains.

We've a muster of 170 men. We have collected more gold than I expected. We can now charter a ship and sail north.

Na na na na na!

I don't know what you're playing at, little girl. But whatever it is, nothing's going to make me leave my post.

Huh?

Good evening.

I've brought you some cakes.

From what we know, there will be some fighting to do. Some of us will die, but we ain't coming back without our kids.

That child, Lord Faa. The police are searching our boats. There's a move in Parliament to rescind our ancient privileges to the waterways. Who is this child that we should come to such a pass?

This girl is the daughter of Lord Asriel. In case any of you have forgotten, he saved Sam Broekman when he was captured by the Turks.

He passed the law allowing our boats to use the kingdom's canals. He fought alongside us, day and night, during the great flood, and saved the Koopman family from drowning!

Have you forgotten, Raymond? And how is your thigh?

You can count on my support.

And now Lord Asriel is being held prisoner in the ice fortress of Svalbard. Do you need me to describe the creatures who are guarding him there?

I said it's fine!

Lord Faa ...

... don't you think women might be needed during the expedition, to look after the children once they've been freed?

I appreciate your courage, Nell, but we'll have little enough space as it is.

But supposing you need women, in disguise as guards or nurses, to help rescue the children?

Well, I hadn't thought of that. We'll consider that most carefully.

We hear about children with no heads, or cut in half and sewn together, and things too awful to mention. I hope you're going to take powerful revenge.

Nothing will hold me back ...

... except judgment.

Once the children are safe, rest assured that it will be time for punishment....

We shall strike the strength out of them, and leave them broken and shattered.

MY HAMMER IS THIRSTY FOR BLOOD, FRIENDS!

WHAT?!

What are you doing here?!

No women, you say?

You have already played your part, Lyra!

But I haven't done anything yet! I want to come north, to rescue my friend Roger and the other children.

I'll tell you what—I'll bring you back a walrus tusk. That's a promise.

But ... this is why I ran away from Mrs. Coulter!

Lyra, there en't no question of taking you into danger.

Don't get any ideas. You're staying here, safe.

But I'm learning how to read the alethiometer. It's coming clearer every day.

You're bound to need that!

THE ANSWER IS NO! NOW GO!

What?! How did you get in?

We will go. Just let 'em try to stop us. We will!

Or I could hide in one of their canoes, or in one of the food crates.

That won't work either.

I don't know if we can do this, Lyra. They'll be watching us like hawks.

Where are we going, Farder Coram? Can I leave my cabin?

No, Lyra.

You must stay hidden. Your mother has all the spies in the kingdom searching for you. By keeping on the move, we'll keep them from finding you.

But we have our spies too, don't we?

There's no hiding anything from you, child.

In fact, we are going to meet our spies at the next stop.

I'm making more progress with the alethiometer, you know....

It won't matter, Lyra. John Faa is not going to let you join the expedition.

No?

Then ... where is the famous book that explains all the symbols?

Ha! You! Once you get an idea in your head ...

It's in Uppsala.

Look, Farder Coram: what does the hourglass mean? The big hand keeps returning to it.

There's often a clue if you look close. What's that little thing on top of it?

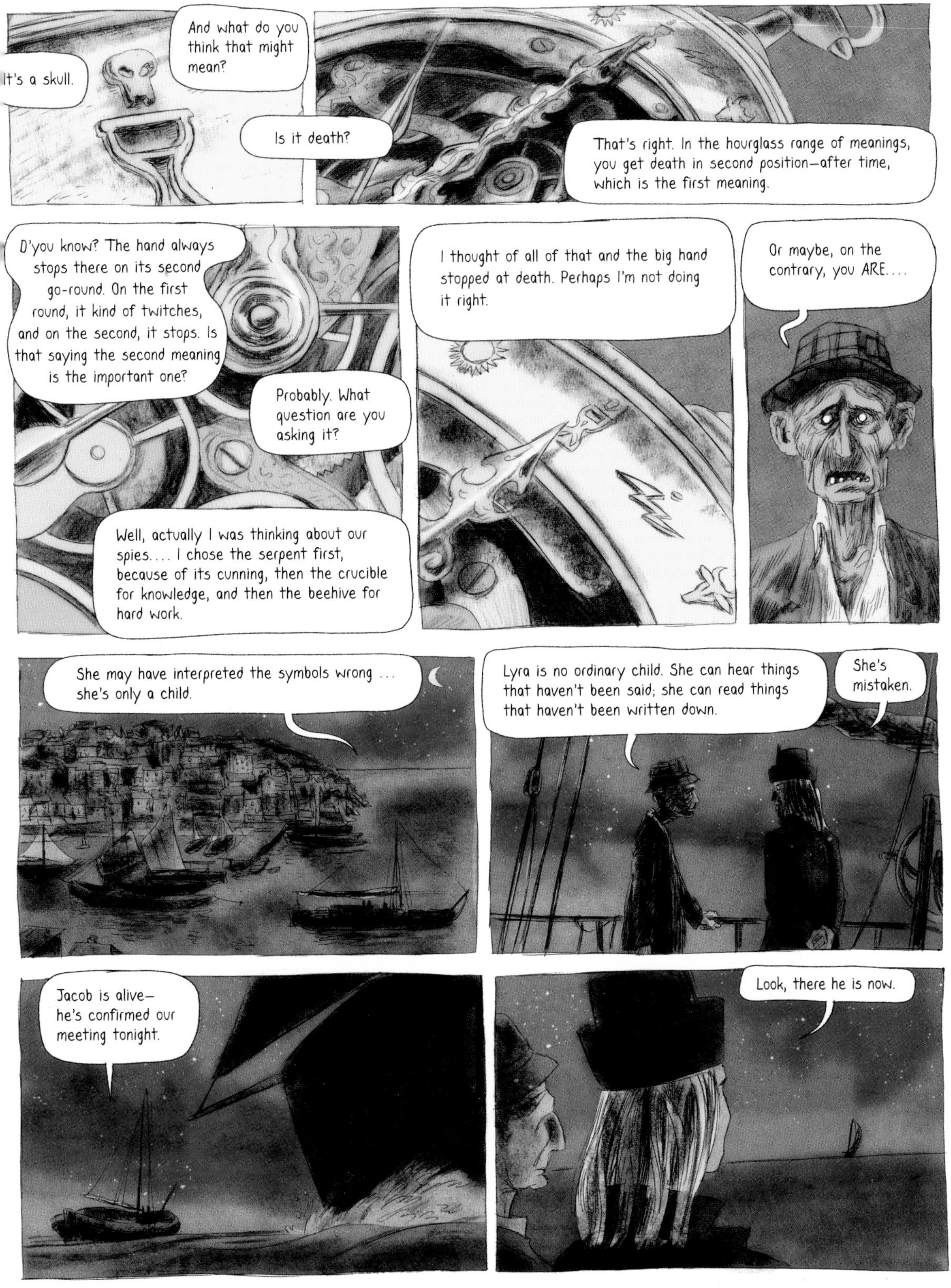
It's a skull.
And what do you think that might mean?
Is it death?
That's right. In the hourglass range of meanings, you get death in second position—after time, which is the first meaning.
D'you know? The hand always stops there on its second go-round. On the first round, it kind of twitches, and on the second, it stops. Is that saying the second meaning is the important one?
Probably. What question are you asking it?
Well, actually I was thinking about our spies.... I chose the serpent first, because of its cunning, then the crucible for knowledge, and then the beehive for hard work.
I thought of all of that and the big hand stopped at death. Perhaps I'm not doing it right.
Or maybe, on the contrary, you ARE....
She may have interpreted the symbols wrong ... she's only a child.
Lyra is no ordinary child. She can hear things that haven't been said; she can read things that haven't been written down.
She's mistaken.
Jacob is alive—he's confirmed our meeting tonight.
Look, there he is now.

Margaret, where's Jacob?

He's hidden under the blanket at the back of the dinghy. He's hurt.

Jacob ... what happened?

Benjamin, Gerard, and I—we captured a Gobbler.

We were trying to find out who was giving orders for the kidnappings. We questioned him for hours.

Where are the children?

Somewhere in Lapland.

He cracked in the end.

Lord Boreal ... The Ministry of Theology ...

That same evening, we broke into the Ministry.

Maps, plans, letters, we planned to steal the lot.

What if we meet Lord Boreal?

He won't be there. Now silence!

Too bad for him. We must get those documents.

Oh no! He's in his office.

SHRIEEEk!

He's dead. They're all dead. Just as Lyra predicted.

It's not my fault, Lord Faa. All I'm doing is interpreting the symbols.

I know, child.

Looks like you're coming with us to the North, after all.

IF YOU DON'T LET ME OUT, I'M GOING TO GO MAD!

She's right.

For a whole month now, we've been moving from boat to boat.

We want to keep her safe, but we're treating her like a prisoner.

All right, let her out for some fresh air.

At last!

Lord Faa is only allowing you out for an hour.

Tell me more about the alethiometer. Have you learned more? Can it tell you what Mrs. Coulter is doing right now?

Yes, I can find out.

Explain to me what you're doing.

The Madonna represents Mrs. Coulter, and I think of her when I place the first needle in that position.

Then with the second needle, I select the ant, because it's very busy.

Finally I choose the hourglass, because it's got *time* and *now* in its meanings.

But how do you know which are the right symbols, and which meaning?

I see them.

Or rather, I feel them.

Well, I make my mind go down and there's another meaning, and I kind of sense what it is. Then I put 'em all together. There's a trick to it, like squinting to see something better.

It's a bit like climbing down a ladder at night. I put one foot down and then feel for the next rung below it.

What does the big hand say?

First a thunderbolt...

... then the child, the serpent, the elephant

... and then a kind of lizard.

I don't understand. It doesn't make sense. The thunderbolt means anger, the child must be me ... but why the lizard?

I'm starting again!

Oh no, the lizard again!

I don't understand! Everything lines up until the lizard.

The meaning's just out of reach! Why?

Calm down, Lyra. It doesn't matter.

Yes! That's it! I CAN FEEL IT!

AAAGH!

AARGH!

?!

Well done, Sophonax!

Don't let it escape.

A second one! I'll get it!

Missed it!

It's gone!

I saw something like it in Africa....

There's a sort of clockwork mechanism inside with a bad spirit pinned to the spring, carrying an evil spell.

As long as the spirit's inside it, it won't never stop. And if you let the spirit free, it's so monstrous angry it'll kill the first thing it gets at.

I understand better now. The elephant stands for Africa.... But what about the lizard, Farder Coram?

It's not a lizard ...

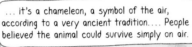

... it's a chameleon, a symbol of the air, according to a very ancient tradition.... People believed the animal could survive simply on air.

Can it be destroyed?

I don't think we can do anything with it.

We'll have to keep it shut up tight in a box and never let it out.

Perfect! Let's throw the devilish thing overboard.

No. The metal would eventually rust, and the devil would come for Lyra wherever she might be. We'll have to keep it with us and keep an eye on it.

But who sent it?

Can't you guess?

You don't need the alethiometer to know the answer.

Mrs. Coulter? But why?

To spy on you, of course. To kill you, perhaps. What a fool I was to allow you up on deck. The one that got away will surely report back to your mother that it's seen you.

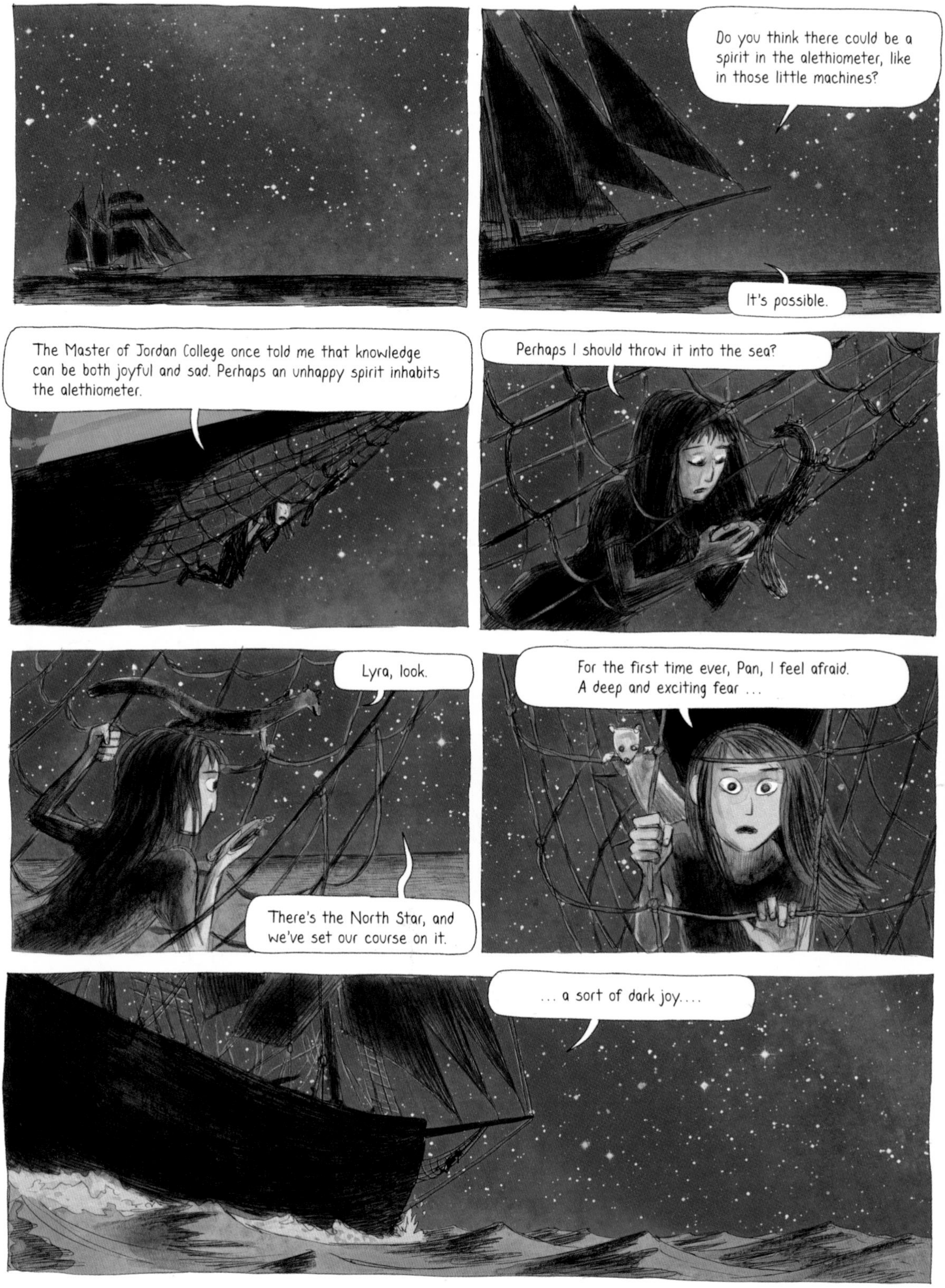
Do you think there could be a spirit in the alethiometer, like in those little machines?
It's possible.
The Master of Jordan College once told me that knowledge can be both joyful and sad. Perhaps an unhappy spirit inhabits the alethiometer.
Perhaps I should throw it into the sea?
Lyra, look.
There's the North Star, and we've set our course on it.
For the first time ever, Pan, I feel afraid. A deep and exciting fear ...
... a sort of dark joy....

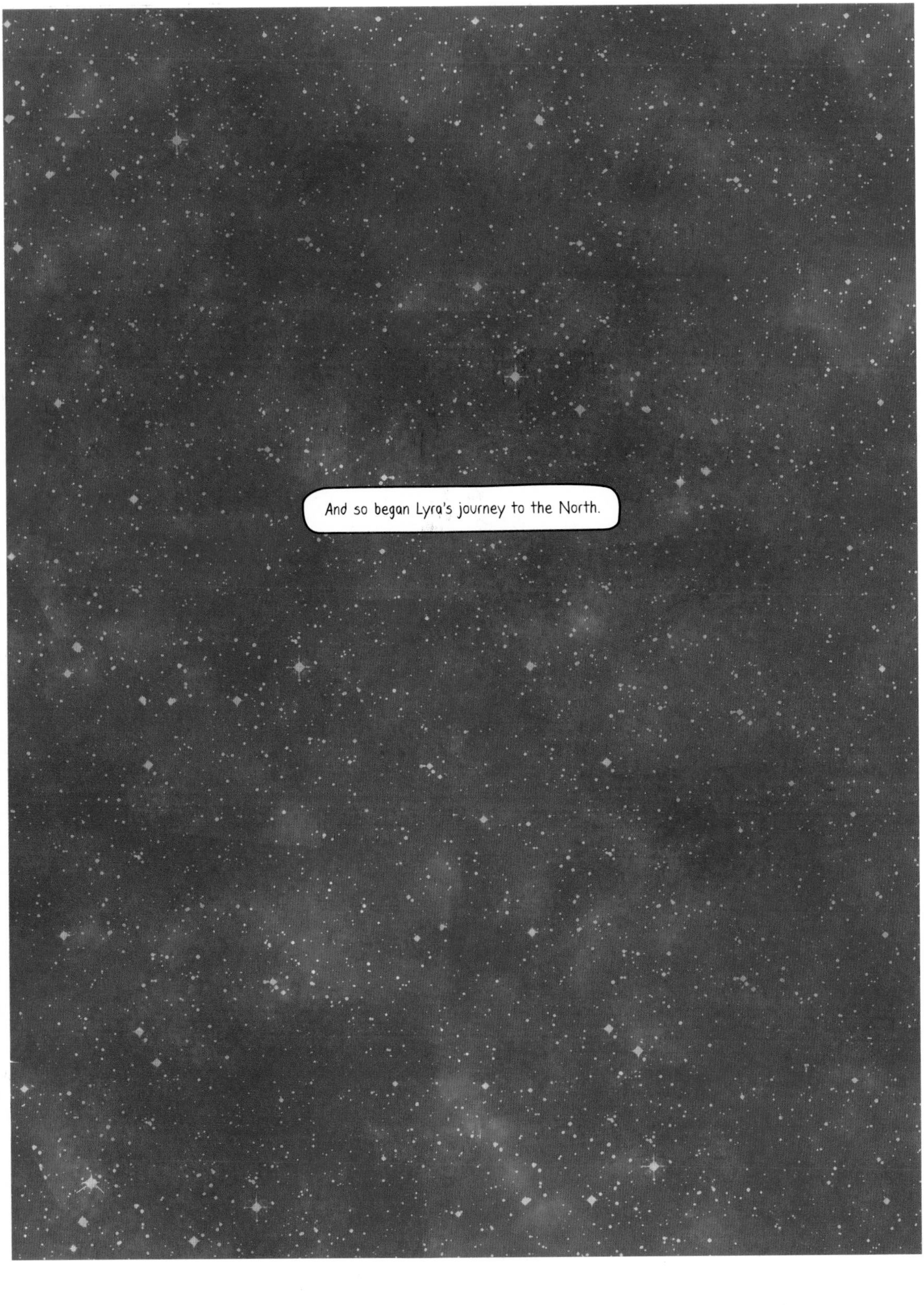
And so began Lyra's journey to the North.

Lyra's journey north will continue in

THE GOLDEN COMPASS
THE GRAPHIC NOVEL

VOLUME 2 coming in September 2016 and

VOLUME 3 coming in September 2017

HIS DARK MATERIALS

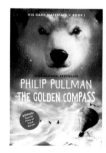   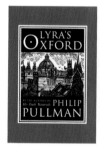 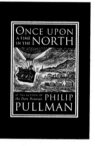

"Pullman's imagination soars. . . . A literary rollercoaster ride you won't want
to miss."
—*The Boston Globe*

"A literary masterpiece. . . . The most magnificent fantasy series since The
Lord of the Rings."
—*The Oregonian*

"Pullman is quite possibly a genius . . . using the lineaments of fantasy to tell
the truth about the universal experience of growing up."   —*Newsweek*